# LANDSLIDE!

The trail was narrow, with a sheer drop below. Gault turned to reassure the girl, but his words died in his throat as a shot echoed through the narrow canyon.

# THE OUTLAWS!

But why were they firing? They were too far behind for anything except a lucky shot. Unless—

*Suddenly Gault realized what the outlaws were doing as bullets slammed into the cliff above, sending down streams of rock and dirt. A low rumbling filled the air.*

# "COME ON!"

he shouted. He jammed his spurs into his buckskin, and he could hear the girl's horse behind him. Faintly, he heard another volley of gunfire—and then all was swallowed up in a vast, roaring thunder!

**⌀ SIGNET** (0451)

# Gun-Slinging Action from Ray Hogan

☐ **THE GUNMASTER.** Aaron Ledbetter... his gun was so deadly they called him The Widowmaker. But when a U.S. Marshal got ready to exchange Ledbetter's life for a kidnapped spitfire and her ransom, The Widowmaker had twenty-four hours to play the deadly doublecross that could win his freedom—or cost him his funeral.

(147529—$2.50)

☐ **OUTLAW'S EMPIRE.** With every man's gun against him, Riley Tabor had to think quick and draw fast. Riley was a cattle driver not a gunslinger—until he had to shoot down a vicious hardcase to save the life of an Eastern greenhorn. Wanted by the law, he headed into territory where no one knew what he had done... and got hired to rid the land of an outlaw army. But is past caught up with him and put him in the middle of a crossfire.... (148274—$2.75)

☐ **THE RAWHIDERS.** Forced outside the law, Matt Buckman had to shoot his way back in. Rescued from the savage Kiowas by four men who appeared suddenly to save him. Matt Buckman felt responsible for the death of one and vowed to ride in his place. Soon he discovered that filling the dead man's boots would not be easy... he was riding with a crew of killers... killers he owed his life to.... (143922—$2.75)

☐ **THE MAN WHO KILLED THE MARSHAL.** He had to force justice from the law—at gunpoint. Dan Reneger had come to the settlement at the edge of nowhere to escape his gunslinging past. But he was in trouble from the start... in a town where the marshal knew his name. (148193—$2.50)

☐ **THE HELL ROAD.** He was carrying a treacherous hostage and a million-dollar coffin through a death trap! He was fair game for Indians, Confederates and bandits, but Marshak was the only man in the Union who could handle this impossible mission—all he had to do was survive. (147863—$2.50)

Prices slightly higher in Canada.

---

Buy them at your local bookstore or use this convenient coupon for ordering.

**NAL PENGUIN INC.**
**P.O. Box 999, Bergenfield, New Jersey 07621**

Please send me the books I have checked above. I am enclosing $_____ (please add $1.00 to this order to cover postage and handling). Send check or money order—no cash or C.O.D.'s. Prices and numbers subject to change without notice.

Name_____

Address_____

City_____ State_____ Zip Code_____

Allow 4-6 weeks for delivery.
This offer is subject to withdrawal without notice.

# TRAIL TO TUCSON

Ray Hogan

224168

DR

CASS COUNTY PUBLIC LIBRARY
400 E. MECHANIC
HARRISONVILLE, MO 64701

A SIGNET BOOK

NEW AMERICAN LIBRARY

Copyright © 1969 by Ray Hogan

All rights reserved

SIGNET TRADEMARK REG. U.S. PAT. OFF. AND FOREIGN COUNTRIES
REGISTERED TRADEMARK—MARCA REGISTRADA
HECHO EN CHICAGO, U.S.A.

SIGNET, SIGNET CLASSIC, MENTOR, ONYX, PLUME, MERIDIAN AND NAL BOOKS *are published by NAL PENGUIN INC., 1633 Broadway, New York, New York 10019*

FIRST SIGNET PRINTING, OCTOBER, 1969

5 6 7 8 9 10 11 12 13

PRINTED IN THE UNITED STATES OF AMERICA

# 1

They broke out of the brush at the upper end of the valley and raced down the slope—two men and a dark-haired girl. In a close knot they swept across the gentle grade, tense, hunched figures silhouetted against the last of the sunlight.

The girl was ahead of the men, one of whom kept his horse directly behind her as if endeavoring to protect her from danger approaching at the rear. From time to time, as they drew nearer the little flinty meadow on the floor of the swale where the opposing slopes converged, each looked back.

Abruptly five more riders spurted from the underbrush, horses straining to overtake those in the lead. The man in front raised his pistol, began to fire. Immediately those with him also opened up, and the girl, features drawn, wide-set eyes bright with fear and anxiety, swiveled her attention to the sharp-faced rider crowding the hindquarters of her horse.

"Nate, they're gaining on us!"

The man shook his head, shouted: "Keep down low!"

She turned back, hunched close to the neck of the tall bay she rode. In that same moment Nate stiffened in the saddle, clawed at the horn to keep from falling. He righted himself, again crouched over his horse, but there was a slackness to him and a broad stain spread below his shoulders. He began to sway. Allowing the reins to fall across the horn, he clutched the horse's flowing mane, flung a despairing glance to the redhaired man little more than an arm's length to his left.

"I'm hit, Morg! Don't tell Lin."

The florid features of the second rider hardened. His heavy lips shaped a curse, and twisting about, he fired twice at the oncoming men, pistol bucking loosely in his hand.

"Ain't got a prayer! Not here in the open."

Nate pointed weakly toward a draw cutting in from their left. It ran straight and narrow for the higher hills to the east.

"In there. Turn. Maybe . . . in the brush and trees."

Morg made no reply, simply shouted at the girl, began to veer in the direction Nate had indicated. Lin, heeding his cry, swerved obediently. The shooting behind them was a steady racket on the evening hush, and now, quartering as they were and offering better targets, the tempo increased.

Sand began to spurt around the thudding hooves of the onrushing horses. Morg flinched as a bullet caromed off his saddle, went screaming into the twilight. He swore again, emptied his revolver at the pursuing riders.

They reached the meadow, crossed its upper edge, the iron shoes of their horses striking fire as they clashed against stone, and gained the narrow mouth of the arroyo.

"Nate's hurt!" the girl cried suddenly, having a glimpse of the man fighting to stay on the saddle. She began to pull in the bay.

"No!" Morg yelled hoarsely. "We got to make them trees, hide in the brush."

She ignored him, continued to slow. Nate raised his arm, and balancing precariously, waved her on weakly.

"I'll—be all right."

White-faced, Lin slackened her pull on the bay's reins, allowed him to pick up the headlong pace. They pounded into the gravel-floored wash, began to buck the clumps of tough sage and rabbit brush crowding in from both sides. Immediately the horses faltered, checked partly by the wall of underbrush, partly by the loose footing.

A yell went up from the pursuing riders. Bullets began to clip viciously through the foliage, shrill off rocks. Morg swore deeply, and now in the lead, flogged his black horse to greater effort.

Abruptly the shooting ceased, indicating they were no longer visible targets. The wounded man raised himself wearily, looked ahead.

"Pull up out of here. They won't expect—"

Whatever else he intended to say was lost in the crashing of his horse through the dry underbrush. But Morg had understood, was swinging his mount to the bank of the wash, goading him savagely up the steep slant for the rim and the tree-covered ridge beyond.

Gaining the crest he wheeled the heaving black. The girl was moving up beside him. Nate had almost made the top. A pistol rapped suddenly from the floor of the arroyo.

"They've spotted us!" Morg shouted, roweling the black into motion. "Come on!"

## 2

Frank Gault, the flat planes of his lean face dark with the glow of sundown, halted on the lip of a shallow basin and stared out over the rolling hills, now gathering a cloak of hazy gold about them as they prepared for the coming night. A few paces away a tiny white and tan gopher, erect as a surveyor's stake, observed him intently, small paws poised at his chest as if preparing to welcome the lone traveler into his private domain.

Gault rubbed at his sweat- and dust-crusted face. As well camp here for the night. It had been a long, hard day for both him and the buckskin. Both needed rest. There was a spring a little ways back up in a side canyon where he could water the gelding and refill his canteen, he recalled; and the basin itself would provide some protection from the wind which was certain to come winnowing in from the distant desert as soon as darkness fell.

He shifted wearily on his saddle. Three more days to Lordsburg, twice that to Tucson, and then the seemingly endless journey from Dodge City would be over. He'd come fast at that, determined this time not to lose out on a job with Jud Weatherby, but it still looked like it was going to be close.

If he failed to get there by the specified date, he could forget, once and for all, ever trying to line up with Weatherby, the largest and best wagon-train operator in the country. He'd tried for years to sign up with the crusty old taskmaster and only last year had gotten his chance.

At the time, he was working for Dale Wilce and had committed himself to stay with the rancher until the trail drive he was heading up was over. Weatherby had sent him word that the job of outrider captain was open and his for the taking.

Frank had accepted at once. Weatherby not only paid the most money but, always in demand, the job was permanent as a gravedigger's. He'd fired off a reply to the wagon master, promising to be on hand on the required date. Then things went wrong on the drive, and he ended up a week behind schedule.

Weatherby hired another man to fill the vacancy and pulled out, leaving word for Gault if and when he showed up, with the stable-owner where the train had assembled. The message was brief and to the point. He took a man at his word, Weatherby said, and depended on him. When that man failed him, that was the end of their relationship.

Later that year Frank encountered Weatherby in Dodge City where he was doing a stint as a special deputy. He again asked for the job if it should open up. He offered no alibis, made no excuses, simply explained he'd made a promise to Wilce and had kept it. A miracle then ensued. Jud Weatherby agreed to give him a second chance.

And so the call had come. He was to join Weatherby in Tucson where a train was shaping up for the long drive to northern California. There'd been considerable outlaw activity reported in the area, Mexicans, Indians, and renegade Americans. It would take a strong man to guard the wagons, get them through. It was the sort of work Frank Gault excelled at, the kind he liked. He'd jumped at the offer, given his promise to be in Tucson in plenty of time.

He'd ridden out of Dodge a day earlier than was necessary, allowing himself ample time, and on the way he made his plans. He'd recruit the men needed for the drive when he reached Tucson. A half-dozen good hands, all experienced and expert with rifle. Such wouldn't take long. The country was full of men on the loose, the majority of whom had undergone army training and service.

This was a trip he was really looking forward to. Only once had he been in the land where gold had been so plentiful, and then for only a short stay. But more than that, he wanted to prove-up to Jud Weatherby. A future with the top wagon master, the assurance of a good job on the trail every year—that was what counted most. And nothing was going to knock him out of his chance to make that dream come true this time ... Nothing ...

But first he had to reach Tucson—and there'd been slight complications en route. There'd been Indian trouble. An affair at Camp Grant, in Arizona, had stirred up the Apaches, got them on the prod all over

Arizona and half of New Mexico. As a result he'd lost a day to roundabout trails. But he still had a little leeway—not much, but enough if he could keep things going right.

Word of the trouble had forced him to change his mind about the number of guards he'd likely need, too. Be smart to double what he'd originally planned on. Chances were he could expect problems all the way to the Colorado.

It was like the time of war, he thought. He'd done scouting duty, putting in three years with Forrest and a brief time with Confederate raider John Mosby. A man learned to move quietly, swiftly, in such days if he aimed to stay alive, and how to do just that he'd learned well.

That experience had served him to great advantage when the hostilities were over. He found scouting and outriding jobs aplenty awaiting him at every hand, varied now and then by a spot of trail driving or serving the law in some town where things had gotten out of control. And with all that his reputation had grown, had reached even to the point where men like Jud Weatherby actually sought him, although Gault, a man of remarkable self-effacement, never realized it.

That he was a loner and not particularly friendly counted for little; that he was a man dedicated to purpose and promise, that he was exceptionally adept with the .44 Winchester carbine that was never out of his reach, and that he knew intimately the trails and byroads that crisscrossed the frontier counted for much —so much in fact that a small legend had begun to grow around him, and pilgrims, bound for distant destinations, felt the better for having him in their party.

He turned then, a sun- and wind-darkened, somewhat brooding man, and made his way back into the pines and lesser growth where the spring lay. The gopher, at his movement, dropped to all fours, scurried into the brush, and disappeared under a ledge.

Brushing his sweat-stained hat to the back of his

head, he glanced to the sky . . . Clear . . . The night would be bright under a moon on its way to fullness. If the gelding hadn't covered so many miles that day, he'd press on for a few more hours, gain a bit of time.

Coming to the lush growth surrounding the hollow where the spring burst forth, he halted, dismounted, stood for a time quietly listening and watching. Assured finally there was no one else around, he led the horse down to the water. Unhooking his canteen, he crossed to the head of the pool. Immersing the container, he allowed it to fill while he sprawled, belly flat, and slaked his thirst.

Around him the sounds of night were beginning to become known, and his senses, attuned to such, recognized and placed each in its proper niche of identification. There was nothing to cause alarm; the moaning of a dove, the rustle of a rabbit, the click of a lizard feeling the temperature's lowering.

There were deer tracks in the soft mud bordering the spring, and not far from those were the prints of a coyote. Springs were popular and necessary places, especially this one so near the arid desert land to the west. Likely it drew its clientele from a considerable distance.

He noted no hoof marks or moccasin tracks, and that afforded him a feeling of relief. But it was nothing he could rely upon, he knew. Apaches would be aware of the springs location, probably used it regularly.

The canteen filled, he rose, stood for a time looking off into the west, wondering at a faint drumming sound, like faraway hoofbeats tapping through the deep hush. At that moment he was a rigid, watchful shape, features composed, dark eyes thoughtful; one corner of his mouth was slightly pulled—souvenir of a Yankee musket ball at Murfreesboro that came within a breath of being too close. Not an unusually tall man, he was well balanced with a thick chest and shoulders that were perhaps a bit too wide.

The breeze shifted. His frame relented. The sound

had gone as abruptly as it had come. Stepping back into the leaves and litter a pace, he bent down, obliterated all traces of his presence, and circled to the buckskin. Leading him off, he removed also the marks the horse had left, and then turned for the coulee.

It would be a good place for a camp, well away from the water. The spring belonged to all manner of life, and no one had the right to make it his personal possession even for so short a time as one night. Such would deprive the wild things of its use as none would approach while he was there.

Mounting, he rode the short distance to the small basin. The country had enjoyed a wet season, he noted absently. Everything appeared moist, well nurtured. Grass would be belly high for the ranchers. Should stop their complaining for a while.

He reached the hollow, swung down. Again he froze, cocking his ear into the stillness. Hoofbeats for sure. No doubt this time. Several horses, running hard. Apaches? Possible, but he doubted it. Only iron shoes would set up a hammering that would carry so far. The noise was coming from the valley beyond the ridge ahead, and that was a considerable distance. Sound fooled you at that altitude, however; it could be coming from even farther.

He continued to listen, again lost the drumming as the wind changed. But he was thinking more about it; the beats had been nearer, more definite, lending strength to the idea that whoever or whatever it was, could be drawing nearer.

The inner caution within him stirred. Maybe it would be better to pull back deeper into the pines where it was wilder and there was a multitude of small draws and canyons that would afford good cover.

He swung about, studied the darkening slope. He'd best do that, run no chances on encountering delay. This time he'd not be late for his appointment with Jud Weatherby. Suddenly he stiffened as gunshots rippled across the silence. Not one gun—several. A half-dozen, perhaps, all racketing steadily. The hoofbeats were pronounced now, clear and sharp—and coming his way.

An impatient anger seized him, pulled his face into a frown of exasperation. Carbine in hand, he swung back onto the buckskin. Why the hell did trouble have to show up—he broke off the thought, swore at his own peevishness. What was eating him? If someone was in trouble, it was only right—in fact he was obligated to lend a hand.

Touching the gelding with spurs, he moved out of the coulee, pointed for the ridge. He'd be able to see what it was all about from there. If it was just the army giving chase to a bunch of renegade Apaches, he'd forget it, stay clear. The army could take care of itself.

But if it was a party being attacked by Indians, he'd do what he could, regardless of personal inclinations. Apaches were everybody's concern in this country, and no self-respecting man refused to go to the aid of another when he was in a tight.

He crossed a narrow saddle, approached the slight hogback from its lower end. Hoofbeats were loud now, mingling with the dry rattle of brush, the clatter of rock. He realized the persons under attack were coming up the opposite side of the hill, bearing straight for him. Immediately he angled to his right, ducked in behind a stand of juniper.

The shooting had ceased, but somewhere back toward the valley there was shouting. It didn't sound like the howls of Indians, more like white men yelling back and forth. He considered that briefly, hauled around sharp as a loud crashing below the crest of the ridge drew his attention. He could hear a horse digging hard to gain the top, grunting, blowing, hooves pounding, and along with that the creaking of leather. Abruptly horse and rider lunged into view.

He was a thickset, bull-necked man with red hair. His florid features were taut; his lips had pulled back over his teeth, and his small eyes were narrowed almost to closing. Bloody streaks on the flanks of the black he rode attested to the urgency of the moment.

Another horse broke over the crest, this one a big bay with flaring nostrils and the whites of his eyes showing starkly. A girl crouched on the saddle, gripped the horn with both hands. Desperation distorted her features, turned beauty into an ugly mask. Reaching the summit, she straightened, looked back.

A third horse bounded over the rocky rim, going to his knees in the effort. A man was clinging to the animal's long mane. When the horse almost fell he slid to one side. Gault saw the wet stain that darkened his shirt.

Hesitating no longer, he spurred out of the brush, wheeled in front of the girl. She jolted with fear at his sudden appearance, and then he saw hope leap into her eyes.

"Help us! Please!" she cried, fighting to settle down the bay. "Outlaws!"

Frank Gault took one look at her stricken features, another at the wounded man, and charged past her, pointing to the ridge.

"Up there! I'll try to turn them . . . Follow."

The girl flung him a grateful look, whirled away. The redhead swung in beside her, both pausing long enough to let the wounded man get in front of them, and then all three pounded for the band of trees at the upper end of the slope.

Gault struck directly for the lower edge of the hogback over which the three had come. The outlaws would not be far behind—down in an arroyo as he recalled the area. If he could catch them there before they started up the steep bank, chances were good he could stop the pursuit.

# 3

Gault reached the crest, hauled up short. Below in the deep shadows he could hear the slap and crackle of brush, the sound of dislodged, spilling gravel. The outlaws had reached the arroyo, were turning to the slope.

He lifted his rifle, poured six bullets into the void, swung the buckskin to one side. Yells lifted, and two or three answering shots rang out.

"Duck into them rocks!" a voice shouted hoarsely. "They've holed up!"

Moving farther to his right, Frank dismounted, tied the gelding to a small cedar. Crouched in the darkness, he listened to the muted noise of the men walking carefully about on the floor of the wash. Getting their position established in mind, he began to work downgrade, circling wide.

"Bryte, stay with the horses."

"All right, Jude."

Gault paused, gauged the position of the speakers. The first would be ten yards or so to his left, near the foot of the slope. Bryte and the horses were below him. Probably at the head of the arroyo.

He continued on, wishing the redheaded rider had stayed behind to lend a hand. Someone to hold the outlaws' attention from the opposite side would have made the plan he had in mind much easier to effect.

Reaching the bottom of the grade, he felt the sandy floor of the wash under his feet, again halted. Four of the outlaws were above him now. He could hear the

15

dry rasp of their labored breathing, the scrape of their boots. All were working their way to the hogback, believing the girl and her companions had taken refuge in the brush and rocks.

Hunched low, keeping to the black shadows, Gault doubled toward the wash, eyes searching for Bryte and the horses. The moon, now that the last of the sunlight had gone, was making its presence known, and the land was bright with a strong, silver glow.

He saw Bryte a moment later. The man was hunkered beside a large rock, the reins of the five horses in his left hand, face turned toward the slope. Somewhere above him a stone dislodged, bounced noisily down until it struck bottom. A voice swore feelingly, another grumbled a reply. Gault eased forward, taking each step with care.

One of the horses sensed his coming, shifted nervously. Bryte yanked on the leathers, half turned. In that same instant Frank stepped from the darkness. He swung the carbine in a short arc. The stock caught the outlaw on the side of the head, cracked sharply. Bryte dropped to the ground and the horses shied away.

"Pete, everything all right down there?"

Gault took a deep breath. "Sure," he replied, imitating the outlaw's voice as best he could.

"What's bothering the horses?"

Gault moved to a position between the slope and the jittery animals.

"Nothing . . . Maybe a rabbit."

Immediately a different voice said: "Hell, that ain't Pete! There's somebody else down there!"

Frank, the horses below him, triggered a shot into the night. Instantly the animals bolted, went thundering off down the arroyo for the distant valley. Shouts sounded on the slope, and Gault, wheeling, rushed for the undergrowth to his left.

"Horses—stampeding! Come on—"

Frank grinned, hurried on, hearing the heedless crashing of brush and sliding of loose rock and sand as the outlaws abandoned the slope to return to the arroyo. But he did not stop to watch; it wouldn't do to let one of them get between him and the buckskin.

The thought came too late. He heard a noisy crashing directly above him, saw the squat bulk of a man appear in his path. Startled, the outlaw pulled up short. Off balance on the steep grade, he teetered precariously, then plunged forward.

"Here!" he yelled. "Over here!"

Gault, feet solidly planted and with all the advantage, sidestepped the man's downward rush. A pistol blasted into the night, the bullet striking stone somewhere beyond him and screaming off into the night.

The outlaw lunged by. Frank struck again with the carbine. The blow caught the man across the shoulders, added impetus to his stumbling descent, knocked him sprawling headlong into the brush.

Gault moved off like a swift shadow, making almost no sound at all. The other outlaws were shouting questions as they scrambled down the slope, demanding replies. Another gunshot racketed, arousing a fresh sally of rebounding echoes and bringing forth an angry response from the darkness.

"Goddammit, it's me! Watch where you're shooting!"

Frank reached the crest, hesitated briefly to get his bearings. The buckskin would be to his right. Spinning, he trotted to where the horse waited. Cautious voices were coming from the foot of the slope directly below him, and jerking the reins free, he swung to the saddle. Off, toward the lower end of the arroyo he could hear a steady drumming. The horses were still in flight.

The outlaws would forget their chase now, at least for a while. They'd be spending the next few hours rounding up their mounts. Roweling the buckskin, he headed up the long grade parallel to the hogback, aiming for the ridge.

The heat of the moments was gone, and suddenly he was having thoughts as to what he'd bought into.

Someone else's trouble—one thing he'd vowed not to do. It appeared he'd inherited a girl, a wounded man, and another who evidently didn't care too much for a fight.

He spat angrily. It could mean lost time—and he had none to spare. If he failed to make it this time on the prescribed date, he could forget about ever working for Jud Weatherby. The old wagon master was not the sort who'd overlook a second breach.

Displeased with himself, with his ill luck, he rode on.

# 4

They were waiting for him within the fringe of the grove, all three still mounted.

"Have they gone?" the girl greeted him in an anxious voice.

Gault nodded brusquely. "They'll be busy for a spell." He ducked his head at the wounded man. "How's he?"

"Bad, I'm afraid. We started to lay him down, decided it best to wait for you. Will they—the outlaws—be back, you think?"

"They will," the red-haired man said. "They ain't letting twenty thousand dol—" He bit off his words, looked down.

Gault was quiet for a moment, then shrugged. "Reckon that's your answer."

The girl glanced to the suffering man on the black next to her. "Then what can we do?" she asked in a strained way.

"Move out of here," Gault said. "They'll know about where to look for you."

Kneeing the buckskin forward, he took up the reins of the wounded man's horse. "Keep up close," he said to the girl, and then swung his eyes to the redhead.

"Bring up the end—and don't be afraid to use that gun you're packing. Would've been a help, back there in the arroyo. The two of us might've stopped that bunch for good."

His words were sharp, his manner curt. The squat rider stirred. "Figured with Nate hurt bad, I'd best stay with Lin."

Lin . . . that was the girl's name. Nate was the man who'd been shot. Frank stared at the stocky rider. "What do I call you?"

"Morg. Morg Benson. Partner there's Nate Cooper. She'd Belinda—Lin. His sister."

"All right, Morg, keep an eye open."

Benson bobbed his round head. "But if they ain't anywheres close—"

"Outlaws aren't the only ones running loose in this country," Gault said bluntly, and moved on.

Lin swung in behind Nate's black. Benson held back until the line had formed and then took up his position.

"You talking about Indians?" he asked.

"Apaches," Frank answered, picking out a faint path that bore directly into the higher hills.

Nate Cooper groaned deeply. The girl drew abreast of him hurriedly, peered closely at his blanched face. She raised her eyes to Gault.

"He's in terrible pain. Will we have to go far?"

"Got to get off the main trail . . . A mile, maybe."

"I—I don't think he can stand it."

Gault shrugged with impatience. Cooper would have to stand it. "Won't take long."

The moon was at full strength now, and the world around them was bright with its glow. Coyotes barked in the distance, and once, overhead in a thickly needled pine, a bird chirped sleepily at their passing.

The path began to veer south, but Gault continued on, ignoring the change, winding in and out of the trees and oak brush, skirting mounds of rock until he came finally to a low, rough-faced bluff. There he swung north a short distance, crossed a brief, grass-covered saddle, and led the party down into a small clearing enclosed on all sides by rock and thick growth.

"Can rest here," he said, pulling to a halt.

Lin was off her horse and at the side of her brother before he could dismount. Moving quickly, he crossed to her, and taking the injured man carefully under the shoulders, lifted him from the saddle. The girl had acted swiftly when he took over, now had a blanket spread on the damp ground. Gently, Gault placed Cooper on it.

Nate grinned weakly up at him. "Obliged. About as far—as I could go."

"You'll be all right after a bit," Lin said, bending over him, fussing with the folds of the blanket.

Nate Cooper shook his head. "Don't bother . . . I'm all right—leastwise, as all right as—I can be."

"Don't talk like that!" the girl scolded. "Soon as you rest you'll be able to go on."

Cooper mustered his wavering smile again, shifted his eyes to Frank. "Never heard—you speak your—name."

"Frank Gault."

"Gault . . . Appreciate—your help."

It had been a matter in which he'd had no choice, Frank thought. If he'd been a mile off in any other direction he wouldn't be standing there now, sweating out the minutes wondering if he was going to lose out on a good job because of them. But he made no mention of it, said instead:

"Better let me have a look at that hole in your back."

"No need," Cooper replied slowly. "Bullet must've nicked—artery. Feel like—I'm filling up."

Lin Cooper's head dropped forward. She began to

sob quietly. Nate pawed about with an unsteady hand, found her arm.

"Now, Lin—none of—that."

Cooper's tongue was growing thick. The words he managed to utter were indistinct. He'd probably assessed his wound correctly, was bleeding to death inside. Gault had seen plenty of such during the war. Nate had an hour, perhaps less, of life to live.

"Gault—"

Frank hunched beside the dying man to catch his words. "Right here."

"A—favor—please?"

Anger and frustration rushed through Gault, making him slow to answer. Finally, "Sure."

"Get Lin—my sister—to the next town . . . Morg, too. Feel better—knowing—you'll see to it."

Frank studied his hands thoughtfully. His shoulders stirred. "All right."

"Be glad to pay," Morg Benson said, mistaking Gault's hesitation. "Whatever's reasonable—"

Frank gave the redhead a withering look. "No charge," he said coldly.

The ragged smile tugged at Nate Cooper's bloodless lips again. "Don't—hold it against—Morg . . . Means well. Good—man."

Lin pressed his hand between hers. "You ought not talk. Save your breath."

"Why? Won't need—breath—where I'm going. Feel like—talking. There water—handy?"

Gault rose, strode to the buckskin and obtained his canteen. Handing it to Lin, he returned to the edge of the clearing, glanced over the long slope. The growth was dense and he could not see far, but all appeared quiet.

"Better—lots better," Cooper was murmuring as he moved back to the man's side. He stared up at Frank, focusing his eyes with difficulty.

"We're mining—people . . . Colorado. Been at it years—many years. Since—the war . . . Morg and me

—doing the mining. Was Lin—kept house—cooked."

Cooper choked, clutched at the canteen. The girl assisted him to drink. He sank back. "Finally got—a stake. Was heading for Arizona . . . New territory. Figured to—get in business—some kind."

"It's your stake those outlaws are after," Gault said.

Nate frowned. "After—it." He stirred, struggled to pull himself up. "Was a—mistake—Morg! A mistake . . . We—never should've—"

"With a little luck we'd have made it," Benson broke in disgustedly. "Just a little luck. That's all we needed. But we still will, Nate, with Gault looking after us. Don't fret none about it. And not about Lin, either. She'll be fine."

"Glad to hear—that . . . Always—had it hard. Never easy for—her . . . Lin—wish I—could've done—more."

"I wouldn't have it any other way," the girl cried softly. "Only, it seems so cruel, so unfair! Just as we were—you—"

"Don't—spill no tears—over me . . . Can figure I got—you—set. Morg—a good man . . . You'll—be happy."

"Promising you that, Nate," Benson said.

Cooper sighed deeply, stared up at the velvet sky littered with diamonds. "Fine—fine night—for dying." His brow pulled into a frown. "Those—men . . . Where—"

"Off in the valley somewhere," Gault said. "Chasing down their horses."

Cooper's features relaxed. "All—the way—from home—Colorado . . . Never spotted—us . . . Then —close—they catch up. How—things go—funny." A tremor rocked him. Again he tried to sit up.

"They—they won't—find us—here? Not—here, Gault?"

"No chance," Frank replied, pressing the man back gently. Nate Cooper's time had about run out. His voice was husky. His words, barely distinguishable, came with great effort.

"Luck—you came—along . . . Been—all over—for us."

Lin had begun to weep again. Beyond her in the half-dark of a shadow, Morg Benson struck a match to the cigarette he'd rolled. The only sound in the hush was Cooper's labored breathing, the distant yapping of a coyote. Or was it a coyote? Gault wondered.

"Morg!" Cooper called suddenly. "Morg!"

Benson stepped forward quickly. "Right here, Nate."

"Leaving—Lin—to you . . . Take care of—her. Depending—on you to—see . . ."

The words trailed off as another spasm shook the man. Benson leaned forward, endeavored to catch the utterances. Gault stared at the mining man's slack features, shook his head.

"He's dead," he said quietly.

# 5

Lin Cooper sobbed quietly over the still figure of her brother for several moments. Benson moved up, took her by the shoulders, drew her to her feet.

"Never mind," he said in a low voice. "I'll look after you, like Nate told me."

The girl did not yield to him, nor did she pull away, simply remained rigid, eyes downcast, a slim shape in the pale light.

"He'll need burying," Morg said unnecessarily.

The girl raised her glance to Gault. "I wish he could

have a church service—all that goes with it. But I guess it's too far to Lordsburg."

Gault nodded.

She looked off over the slopes. "Here will be all right. He loved the mountains. I expect he'd rather have it this way."

Frank moved up to Cooper's side, faced her. "If you'd like to wait up there in the rocks—" he said hesitantly.

Lin knelt over her brother. "We Coopers take care of our own," she replied. "I'll look after Nate if you'll do the rest."

They had nothing with which to dig. Searching about, Gault located a hollow place beneath a bluff, and using sticks, he and Morg Benson further deepened the depression. After that they collected a number of stones and turned then to Lin.

She had wrapped the blanket around her brother, secured it with lengths of cord. As Gault and Benson approached, she stepped back, waited while they carried the body to the hollow and lowered it into place.

Frank moved off, prepared to let the girl have her last moments of grief. Benson, unthinking, began to push the loose soil piled along the grave's edge in upon the shrouded shape. Frank caught the man by the arm.

"Time we had a look at the trail," he said gruffly.

Morg stared, flushed deeply, and followed him to the edge of the clearing. Lin knelt by her brother, bowed her head, a small, dejected figure in the streaming moonlight. Morg Benson studied her from the distance.

"Sure hard on her."

Gault made no reply. He had no liking for Benson, although he could name no specific reasons as to why he felt that way. Something about the man just seemed to rub him wrong.

"But she'll be fine," Morg continued. "I'll be seeing

to that. Fact is, we're figuring to marry up soon as we get to a proper place."

Frank stirred, his gaze lost on the hills . . . It would be the best thing for the girl even though he didn't particularly care for her choice of husband. The frontier was no place for a lone woman, especially one so young and attractive as Lin Cooper. And wealthy . . . But he was wondering how she felt about Benson. He had seen no indication on her part that such an arrangement was in the offing—and to her liking.

"She feel that way?"

Benson's brows arched belligerently. "Sure she does! Been the deal all along. Nate sort of—"

"Maybe it was Nate's idea, not hers."

Morg rubbed at the stubble on his chin. Even in the silver light his skin had a reddish cast.

"Well, she never said nothing against it. What's making you so interested?"

Gault shrugged at the stiffening in the man's tone. "I'm not."

"And you damned well better keep it that way!" Benson snapped, suddenly angry. "This here's my business, understand? Stay out of it!"

Features cold, expressionless, Frank Gault wheeled slowly. "That's a habit of mine, but anytime a man starts laying down the law to me, he—"

"I—I guess I'm ready."

Lin's voice reached Gault, ended his words before he was finished. Brushing by Benson, he returned to the grave, began to fill it in. Morg joined him, and together they quickly covered the body and piled the rocks upon it.

The girl, with a small cross fashioned of tightly-lashed tree branches in her hand, stood quietly by until they had finished and then stepped forward, implanted the crude marker at the head of the rocky mound.

"It isn't much, Nate," Frank heard her murmur, "but I won't forget."

Gault turned back to the center of the clearing.

He'd participated in the same scene dozens of times during his trips back and forth across the land west of the Mississippi, and the irony of it forever moved him to impatience.

It seemed always the wrong persons: the truly good and decent folk were the ones who found a final resting place in some lonely, desolate spot along the way. The outlaws, the kill-crazy renegades and gunslingers, were either hanged in a town after trial or else toted in across a saddle by the law or some reward-seeking bounty hunter, to end up later in a quiet church graveyard where a softhearted preacher spoke kind words over them . . . But the people who mattered—

"Mr. Gault, I want to thank you."

Again the girl's voice broke into his thoughts. He nodded to her. "No need. Wish we could have done more."

"We did all we could. Nate would understand. What happens now?"

"Your brother wanted me to take you to Lordsburg. Expect that's—"

"Won't be needing you," Morg Benson broke in, stepping up beside Lin. "I figure we can make it without any help."

The girl turned to him in surprise. "But I thought you wanted—and Nate said—"

"Been doing some thinking about it. We'll just let Gault here go on his way. I'll handle things."

Frank shrugged. The idea of not being delayed after all appealed to him; but Benson was a fool and he had the girl to think of. Besides, he'd given his word to the dying Nate Cooper.

"Lordsburg's closer by the valley road," he said, ignoring the man. "We head back that way we're bound to run into those outlaws. We stay on the trail it'll take a day longer, but our chances of shaking them are good."

Morg Benson, his face angry, took a half-step forward. "Just hold up a minute now! I reckon I've got something to say about this!"

"Far as you're concerned, you can do as you damned well please," Gault replied evenly. "Head out on your own, if you like. The lady stays with me until I can get her to Lordsburg."

A sly grin crossed Benson's lips. "Wouldn't be thinking about all that money we're carrying now, would you?"

Frank clung to his temper, shook his head. "Fact is, I'm thinking about the day I'll be losing that could cost me a good job. But I said I'd see her through, and I will."

"That's the way it will be, Morg," Lin said quietly. "If you want to go on alone, it's up to you. But you don't know this country, and there are Indians, and those outlaws—"

"I'd get by," Benson said sullenly. After a moment he asked: "Where else this trail go?"

"Runs from here to Bear Mountain, angles off to the Burros—another range. Goes through a place called White Rock Canyon and then into Lordsburg. No other towns in between."

"How long'll it take?"

"Four days—with luck."

Lin sighed. "So far . . . seems months we've been on the road."

"Lordsburg's a pretty good town. Stagecoach service there. Connections going east, west, wherever you want to go."

"Not east—there's no reason. Maybe on west."

"We'll do like we figured," Benson said firmly. "Go right on to Arizona. Only difference'll be it's me and you now that Nate's gone."

Evidently Morg had decided his best chances were to stay with the party. It didn't matter to Frank Gault as long as he posed no problems. There was still hope of reaching Tucson in time if he pressed hard. Lin

Cooper's words threw doubt upon the possibility of a swift, untroubled passage in that next moment.

"I don't know, Morg," she said. "When we get there we'll talk about it."

Benson's head came up sharply. A frown pulled at his broad features. "The hell—we're doing what I say!"

The girl turned away deliberately, placed her back to him, faced Gault.

"Could I rest for just a little before we go on? I'm so tired, I—"

Frank picked up his rifle, cradled it in his arms. He was impatient to get moving, allow the five outlaws no opportunity to cut down the distance separating them now that the matter was his responsibility. But the girl was beat. It showed in her eyes, in the lines of her face. He'd as well get used to it—to delays, slow travel, and all else that came with having a woman on his hands.

"Guess we can spare a little time," he said begrudgingly. What they both seemed to overlook was that it was all for their sake, not his.

"Thank you," she murmured, and then as he moved off, "Will you be near?"

He pointed to the edge of the clearing. "Up there where I can keep an eye on the trail."

She gave him a worn smile, turned, began to remove her blanket from her saddle. Benson eyed her angrily for a time, spat, walked stiffly to his horse for his bedding.

Gault considered the man's rigid frame briefly, continued up the slight grade. The redhead hadn't offered to share sentry duty with him, but he reckoned Morg Benson wasn't that kind of a man, even when it was his neck that was at stake.

# 6

Irritable, Frank Gault reached the upper end of the open ground and halted. He could not see the section of trail immediately below him from that point, only a strip of fair length a considerable distance farther down the slope.

There was no one in sight, but being a man who took nothing for granted at such times, he moved off through the brush, made his way to where he could look upon that portion not visible to him from above. He gave it careful study, and then finally satisfied no one was in the area or had passed that way, he retraced his steps to the edge of the clearing.

He doubted the outlaws were anywhere near yet. It would take time to recover the horses, all of which had apparently run until they reached the valley with its deep grass, well beyond the mouth of the arroyo. The chore could consume hours.

He hoped so. Not only was Lin Cooper near exhaustion both physically and emotionally, but more—the horses, his own included, needed rest. Thinking of the animals, he hoped Morg Benson had loosened the saddle cinches; they should receive the best care possible to preserve their strength.

He was beginning to feel the need of sleep himself. It had been a long day and a none-too-easy one as he had cut direct across the Beaverhead country, and the going had been hard. Sleep, or the lack of it, never bothered him too much, however, being accustomed to taking his rest when and where he could—and then never releasing fully his consciousness.

Thus the faint scuff of a boot behind him alerted him instantly. He turned, saw Lin Cooper, blanket draped across her slim shoulders, coming toward him through the brush. In the cool light her features were pale, wan, and her wide-set eyes looked swollen.

She faced him apologetically. "I guess I'm too tired to sleep," she said and sat down beside him.

"Happens."

"So much in my mind . . . I thought maybe—if I talked to someone—"

Her brother's death, the outlaws, the danger through which she was passing, the friction between her and Morg Benson—it was not difficult to understand why she was overwrought. Gault felt himself soften toward her.

"Fine night," he said, glancing to the sky, hoping to make it easier for her.

"It is. Like in Colorado. Sometimes the stars were so low you could almost touch them."

"Colorado. Like it there . . . Where was your home before that?"

"Sharpsburg. That's in Maryland."

Gault nodded, and had his own moment of personal memories . . . Antietam . . . Stone bridges . . . Smoke boiling through the cornfields . . . The unnerving crash of cannonballs.

"I know. Saw a bit of the war there."

"You did? Nate did, too. He was an officer with General Hooker. At Antietam Creek. Got wounded, but worst of all, our home was near and he had to stand by and watch while guerrillas burned it to the ground."

"Nothing's ever good about a war."

"The terrible thing was that my folks were in the house at the time it started. Nate thought I was there, too. He worried about it but there wasn't anything he could do. It wasn't until weeks later that he learned our parents had died in the fire. Only reason I didn't was because I'd gone to a neighbor's."

"Everything lost?"

"Everything," Lin said, staring across the rolling, silver-flooded slopes with their shadow-filled hollows. "After that I lived with those neighbors, the Masons, until Nate was discharged and came for me. He was very bitter about it all. Said even though we'd won the war, we'd lost.

"He'd decided to move away, get to Colorado and hunt for gold—just the two of us. He'd never leave me alone again, he said—not until I was married and had a husband to look out for me. He blamed himself somehow for what had happened—losing the folks and our home, and neighbors having to put me up. It bothered him a lot and he was always trying to make it up to me, although there was no need."

"No fault of his. Everybody gets hurt, one way or another at times like that."

"I tried to tell him that, but it was no use. It was sort of—well—an obsession with him. Anyway, we moved to Colorado. Went to a place near a town called Central City. Some man he'd met in the army told him he could find gold there. We did find some and that encouraged him, so he filed a claim, or whatever it is you do to make it your property, and then we built a cabin. It was a little, two-room affair but it was nice, warm. We had a lot of snow up there."

"That when you met Benson?"

"I don't know exactly when Nate met him, or even how they got acquainted. Just seems they met, got to talking, and ended up being partners. We added another room to the cabin and Morg moved in . . . They did the mining and I kept house. It was that kind of an arrangement."

"Morg seems to think the partnership is going to continue—the two of you. That the way you feel?"

Lin shrugged, and if she resented the question, she gave no sign. "I guess the idea just sort of grew, us being together so much all those years. And Nate liked the idea. He thought Morg was a fine man."

"And you?"

"Maybe I felt that way back in Colorado, away from everybody, and everything . . . Now I'm not so sure."

"Be a good idea to set him straight," Gault said. "Save yourself a lot of grief later. After what your brother told him there at the last—"

"I know. Nate was thinking of me and what was best. But I'm not sure I see it that way. Once we get to Lordsburg, I'll decide what I want to do. I'll have plenty of money—ten thousand dollars."

"A lot," Frank admitted.

"All in currency—and in my saddlebags. Nate thought it best I carry it. Said if anything went wrong I'd be the most likely to get through."

Gault had wondered about the twenty thousand dollars first mentioned by Benson. It wasn't in gold, he'd realized. Such an amount would have weighed a great deal.

"Good idea," he said. "If you hadn't converted it to paper, you'd need a packhorse, and they can be a big problem."

"That's what Nate said the day he and Morg came home, told me we were moving to Arizona. Said we'd be traveling light, that I needn't take anything except the clothing I was wearing. Since we had plenty of money I could buy all new things once we got there.

"I didn't realize we'd done so well in the mine until he mentioned twenty thousand dollars, but I guess I'd never really thought about it. We were there several years and the two of them worked hard at it every day. Maybe it isn't actually a lot when you add up all the hours of hard labor."

"How'd that bunch of outlaws get in on the deal? Had they been hanging around the mine?"

"Maybe. I don't know. I never saw any of them myself. I think they must have been in the bank when

Nate and Morg turned in the gold for paper money . . . Or maybe they heard about it later."

Gault nodded. "You have any other trouble on your way down—with Apaches, maybe?"

"No, only those men. Are the Indians bad?"

"Pretty much on the prowl since that mess at Camp Grant. Lucky you didn't run into a bunch."

Lin stifled a yawn, drew the blanket more closely about her body, and smiled at Gault.

"Afraid I've been a nuisance, running on and on like I have. But I feel better. Think I can sleep now."

"Glad to hear it. You'll need some rest. Tomorrow'll be a hard day—a long one, I expect."

She looked at him curiously. "When do you sleep, Mr. Gault?"

"Frank," he corrected. "Never takes much for me. Learned to grab my forty winks when I could."

She rose to her feet. "You'll have to call me Lin if I'm to say Frank." She glanced around hesitantly. "Will it be all right if I lie down here—close?"

"Anywhere you like."

The girl sighed, spread her blanket on the ground a few steps from where he sat. He got up, helped her roll herself into the woolen folds. Settled, she smiled up at him.

"Good night, Frank."

Gault bobbed his head, resumed his place on the slight rise. Only then did it occur to him that Lin Cooper, perhaps, feared being alone with Morg Benson.

The first streaks of light were showing in the east when the last of the scattered horses was recovered.

Jude Worley, his stubble of beard caked with sweat and dust, body aching with weariness, hunched over the small fire they'd built on the flat to ward off the morning chill and watched sourly as Anson Pearce brought in the final mount.

They'd located the first one a half mile out in the valley, due west of the arroyo. All five of them had concentrated on it—Hazelwood's sorrel—and eventually managed to grab him. From then on it was up to Pearce, who was the best hand among them with horses, to search each one out, drop a loop over his head, and bring him in. It was a cold, tedious job, and the waiting around wore hell out of a man's nerves.

Worley glanced to Pete Bryte, still nursing his shattered jaw, and studied the man morosely. A bit to his left Link Hazelwood and Rufe Damon sprawled on the sand doing their best to get a little rest.

"Got to find me a sawbones," Bryte said with pain-filled effort. "Thing's giving me fits."

Worley spat. "Nearest place'll be Lordsburg."

"That where we're heading now?"

Worley stared off toward the mountains rising steeply above the valley. The silver sheen that had capped the pines and glistened on the rocks had disappeared, but all below was still dark and in shadow.

"If that's where the trail they're following goes."

Bryte groaned. "Hell, they could be going anywhere! It all right with you if I take out, head straight for Lordsburg?"

Jude Worley shrugged. "All right with me if it's all right with the Apaches."

Pete moaned softly. "Never make it alone . . . God, wished I had a drink."

Jude watched Pearce ride in. Rising then, he crossed to where Hazelwood and Damon lay, nudged them none too gently with his booted toe.

The two men rolled over, got stiffly to their feet. Damon, a thin, graying oldster with a stringy moustache, scrubbed at his chin in disgust.

"Can't you even wait for daylight?"

Worley jabbed his thumb at the eastern horizon. "It's here."

"Ought to take time, make some coffee."

"Later."

"Hell, they'll have holed up! We won't lose nothing."

"Maybe. Ain't taking no chance on whether they did or not."

Pearce muttered something at low breath, chafed the inside muscles of his thighs. Link Hazelwood shrugged, studied the long slope with its massive piles of rock, deep, forbidding canyons.

"Hell of a looking place," he said. "You know the country, Jude?"

Worley wagged his head wearily. "Ain't never been in it, but if they can get through, I can get through . . . Mount up."

# 7

Frank Gault moved off the point upon which he sat, halted beside the girl. He disliked waking her; she was sleeping soundly and had been for over four hours, but the feeling was upon him that to remain there longer was unsafe. Reaching down, he shook her gently.

Lin roused instantly. "What is it? Are they—"

Frank stilled her fear with a raised hand. "Time we pulled out."

She sprang to her feet, and hugging the blanket, started for the clearing a step or two ahead of Gault.

Morg Benson still slept. While Lin awoke him, Frank brought up the horses, noting with a stir of anger that the cinches had not been slackened. He was tempted to say something to Benson about it but passed it off. It was too late now, and he supposed he should not have expected a miner to know much about horses. Next time he'd see to it personally.

"Where you been?"

Benson's question was a peevish growl in the quiet.

"I couldn't sleep," Lin replied. "Sat up and talked with Frank."

"So it's Frank now?" Benson said, his voice rising. "And I reckon he's calling you Lin!"

"Why shouldn't he? It's my name."

"Seems you two got mighty familiar all of a sudden," Morg remarked suspiciously. "How long was you up there, doing that talking?"

"All night," Lin said, suddenly defiant. Wheeling, she crossed to her horse, began to tie her blanket roll to the back of the saddle.

Benson glared at her briefly, spun on his heel, and crossed to where Gault stood. His flushed face was taut with anger.

"Mind what I told you earlier, mister!" he snarled, shaking a finger at Frank. "I don't aim to let you or nobody else—"

"Get out of my way!" Gault snapped, and knocking the man's arm aside, led his horse to the edge of the clearing.

He was having difficulty restraining himself. He would like nothing better than to smash his fist into Benson's sneering, smirking face, knock a few teeth down his throat, but there was no time to spare for matters of personal satisfaction. The chore of getting Lin Cooper to Lordsburg safely, dodging outlaws and roving Apaches en route, all the while fighting the hours to reach the further destination of Tucson and meet with Jud Weatherby, would be about all he could handle.

Impatient, he waited in the brush along the clearing until the girl and Benson were mounted, and then moved off, doubling back through the rocks and clumps of mountain mahogany a short distance above the path they had made in arriving.

With Lin immediately behind him and Morg a short distance back of her, leading Nate Cooper's horse, he followed along the tailings of a bluff running parallel to the main trail, hoping to avoid a junction with it as long as possible. The outlaws would be watching closely for hoof prints; if he could keep the trail clean for a considerable distance, he might create delay, possibly throw them off entirely. The effort was worth the try, he concluded.

They pressed on, progress necessarily slow through the undergrowth. They reached a ragged spill where previous storms had caused the end of a butte to slough, create a steep-sided barrier. Gault dismounted, signaled for the others to do likewise. On foot, they led the horses across the jumbled confusion of rock and dead brush.

"It going to be like this all the way?" Benson demanded when they resumed the saddle. "Thought you said there was a regular trail."

"Right below us," Frank replied.

"Then why'n hell are we—"

"We don't want to leave tracks for those outlaws to follow," Lin explained before Gault could shape an answer.

Frank grinned to himself in the half-dark. Smart girl—this Lin Cooper.

A half mile later they were compelled to rejoin the trail. A solid wall of granite thrust itself from the breast of the slope, and there was no way around except by the established path.

They had covered a considerable distance through the untracked brush, however, and Gault reckoned the outlaws would be slowed to quite an extent, thus allowing them to maintain a good lead. But he'd not bank on it; Lordsburg was a long way off. He'd watch for other opportunities to better their position.

The sun broke over the horizon not long after that, flooding the hills and long canyons with soft light. The air began to warm at once, and the clearness of the sky gave promise of heat to come. Taking into consideration the condition of the horses as well as that of his fellow travelers, he knew he could not expect to cover much ground that day.

But they'd keep going until they reached McMullen Mountain. The animals would be in need of rest by then, and there'd be ample grass along with plenty of water for them. Human wants could be satisfied, too. Chances were good both Lin and Morg had gone without food the previous day as well as the night. He kept forgetting that everyone was not of his turn, taking rest and eating only when the urge was upon him.

He glanced over his shoulder to the girl, pointed to McMullen's towering peak. "We stop there, fix a bite to eat."

She nodded. "If you think it's safe."

They moved on steadily with the sun climbing swiftly on their left. Altitude was keeping the heat down to some extent, and riding through the close standing pines was pleasant. Bright patches of flowers blazed on the open slopes—paintbrush, clusters of yellow crownbeard, purple verbena, and woolly locoweed. Brittlebush stirred in the light breeze, and the tips of wild grass dipped and flowed like a red sea. It had been a wet spring, there was no doubt of that.

They reached McMullen Mountain late in the morning and halted in a hollow where a spring bubbled forth from under a fern-shrouded ledge, cut a shallow path for a dozen yards, and disappeared again into the damp earth.

"I'll be looking after the horses," Gault said to Morg as he swung down. "Get a fire going. Small one. Use deadwood—don't want any smoke."

Benson grumbled something in reply, but Frank, unhearing, turned to removing the saddles and bridles from their mounts. Neck-roping them, he led them to the lower end of the stream. The horses were anxious but he gave them only a short ration, picketed them on a thick stand of grass near the camp. They would have their second helping of water later.

Doubling back to the spring, he found Lin had already obtained food from their meager supply, was busy in its preparation. A small lard tin, filled with water, sat over the flames, heating for coffee. Benson was off somewhere searching for more smokeless wood.

"Won't take long," the girl said without looking up. "It'll be warmed-over dried meat and biscuits."

"Be fine," Gault said. "With luck we'll be able to fix a good meal tonight."

His tone caused her to turn, study him. "There something wrong?"

He shook his head, knelt, poked more twigs under the simmering water.

"I saw you looking back over the way we came. Did you see any sign of those outlaws?"

"Nothing."

She frowned. "Isn't that good—what you want?"

"Maybe," he said shrugging. "Feel better if I had spotted them. Know then just where they are."

Lin resumed her chore of slicing the chunk of beef with a clasp knife, spreading the strips in the spider.

"They must be far behind us," she said.

"Like to know just how far. Expect they're keeping off the trail, same as we did."

She quickened her movements. "Then we'd best hurry. I'll—"

"Can spare an hour," he said, rising, and moved off to where he had piled their gear.

It would be easier on the horses if their loads were lightened, and since they had Nate Cooper's black running with little more than a saddle on his back, it would be smart to make him their pack animal.

Disregarding his own tack, he removed blanket rolls, canteens, the few extra items of clothing, and whatever else was attached to Lin's and Morg's saddles, transferred all to Nate Cooper's rigging. He made one exception: when he came to the girl's saddlebags he recalled what she had said about the money. Best he leave the leather pouches with her. Apparently she felt better with the cash in her care.

The change amounted to only a few less pounds of burden for the horses Lin and Benson would be riding, but the miles that lay ahead of them would be hard ones, especially through White Rock Canyon. Insofar as Cooper's black was concerned, he'd be carrying far less weight than if he had a rider.

Little more than an hour later they were again on the move, still bearing southeast. Gault had no specific point in mind that he hoped to reach by sundown; he sought only to cover as much ground as possible before being forced by darkness to halt. Old, abandoned Fort West was to their left, he remembered, but it was too far off the trail to be of use for a camp; time would be lost in making the detour.

Late in the afternoon Lin's bay picked up a stone, began to limp. She noticed it at once, called Frank's attention to it. He removed the offending obstacle, but the horse continued to favor the hoof, and taking no chances, he switched gear and had her mount Nate's black.

"When we stopping?" Morg Benson wondered when they were again under way. "Ain't hardly been off this saddle since yesterday morning."

Gault swung his gaze to the west. Still a couple of hours of light remaining.

"Sundown," he said.

Benson swore softly. "Man can only take so much," he grumbled. "Can't expect him to keep going on and on—no sleep, no fit grub . . ."

Frank Gault's lips tightened. The necessity wasn't of his making; the outlaws weren't after *him*.

# 8

They halted in a rocky draw a short distance above the trail. There was no convenient spring, but the walls of the slash were steep and the glare of a fire would not be too noticeable.

While Lin and Morg set up the camp, Gault saw to the care of the horses, giving them a little water from the canteens and staking them out on a patch of grass at the head of the wash. They were in better condition than he had figured, and now, after a full night's rest, should be in excellent shape to travel far the next day.

That was a comforting thought. Perhaps they'd be able to reach Lordsburg a day earlier, and he could get Lin and the surly Morg Benson off his hands sooner than he'd hoped. A bit of good luck just might do that for him.

Lin had the fire going and the spider ready when he returned. He stood for a few moments watching her lay strips of salt pork into the cast-iron utensil, and then moved on to assist Benson, scraping dead leaves and grass together for their beds. They'd have a proper camp that night, one where all three could sleep well; they could, assuming the outlaws had gained no ground on them and no Apaches put in an appearance. That was a condition that refused to budge from Gault's mind.

A time later, as darkness claimed the land, they ate their first complete meal—fried pork, beans, hot biscuits, and coffee.

"This is a lonely place," Lin said as they sat by the

fire with their coffee. She glanced about at the hushed, brush-covered slopes, the silent walls of rock, and shivered. "Are we safe here?"

"Safe as we can expect to be on the trail."

"But—what if those outlaws—"

"Aim to have a look from that high point later, see if I can spot their campfire. Apaches are something else. We won't know it if they're around."

"Indians!" Morg spat the word. "You really think there's a chance we could be jumped by them? Sure ain't seen any."

"Plenty of them prowling the country," Frank said curtly. "Reason we're keeping that fire low. Only a fool would send them an invitation."

Lin refilled his cup. "You said they were all stirred up over something. Camp Grant, I think it was. What started it—and where's Camp Grant?"

"It's an army post, down in Arizona. One of the Indian chiefs, name of Eskiminzin, brought his tribe in and surrendered to the soldiers. Said they'd had enough fighting, were ready to live in peace with the whites. They'd been hiding in the mountains for four or five years, barely staying alive. All they wanted was to return to their old village on the San Pedro River.

"The army went for it, gave them grub and blankets and such, sent them on their way, figuring they'd have no more problems with that particular bunch. There were quite a few of them—about two hundred counting all the strays that wandered in."

"Then they double-crossed the army, went back on their promise," Benson snorted. "What else would you expect? Indians are all the same."

Gault shook his head. "No, not quite."

"Any I ever run across was," Morg said.

"If they didn't start trouble, who did?" Lin asked.

Frank took a swallow of his coffee. "Rest of the country was still having trouble. Apaches were raiding and stealing cattle, burning down ranch houses and such. Somebody got the idea that Eskiminzin's people were in on it, fooling the army into thinking they were peaceful but actually doing a lot of the raiding. They figured an Apache was an Apache, and a savage no matter what tribe he belonged to.

"Whole thing ended when a party of a hundred and fifty or so Americans, Mexicans, and Papagos—that's another tribe of Indians—cracked down on Eskiminzin's village. Hit it early in the morning when everybody there was asleep. Killed about half his people, most of them women and kids. Biggest part of the men weren't there. They'd gone out on a hunting party.

"Result was that about every Apache in the country grabbed up whatever weapon he could lay his hands on and's out now looking for the chance to kill himself a few whites."

"Not hard to understand why," Lin murmured. "It was a terrible mistake."

"How do you know it was?" Benson countered. "You said the men were out hunting. Could be they only claimed that to keep the soldiers happy. How do you know they weren't in on those raiding parties?"

"Lot of people believe that," Gault said.

Lin leaned forward. "What do you believe?"

"Met Eskiminzin once. Struck me as an honest man. I don't think he'd lie."

Morg grunted his disgust. "I ain't never seen an honest Indian. Never met one I'd trust from here to the end of my leg."

"About the way everybody feels in the country now, but it makes no difference. Point is, the hills are crawling with Apaches out to avenge a massacre—those who'd been peaceful up to the time, and those who'd never stopped fighting . . . It's a bad situation."

Again Lin Cooper glanced around at the shadows crowding in on the draw. The moon was again strong, but scudding clouds streaked the sky and light, and darkness was a restless, ever-changing thing.

"Do you think there are some of them out there, hiding, watching us, just waiting for a chance—"

Gault smiled. "Doubt it. Don't think we've attracted any attention yet," he said, hoping what he said was truth. But there was no sense in worrying her.

Rising, he kicked dirt on the fire, trampled it thoroughly, and picked up his rifle.

"Be making my bed near the trail," he said, obtaining his blanket. "When you fix yours, lay it close to the brush at the edge of the clearing. Don't want anything left in the open."

He did not bother to explain the reasoning behind the order, not wishing to alarm the girl any more than necessary; but if some wandering Apache brave passed by during the night, he wanted the clearing to look empty.

Rifle in hand, blanket over his shoulder, Frank walked to the lower end of the wash, climbed the embankment to a slight rise where he could look back over the trail. Turning his eyes to the north, he began a methodic probe of the night. A trickle of satisfaction rolled through him.

Far in the distance the red eye of a campfire gleamed through the darkness. It would be the outlaws. There'd be no danger from them that night; the need for rest had overtaken them and their horses, too.

Gault sighed, made himself comfortable. He wished he could be as certain about the Apaches as he was about the five men trailing them.

He roused suddenly from the half-wakeful state into which he ordinarily lapsed while on the trail, the deep tones of a man's voice striking at his consciousness. It was Morg Benson, he realized. Sitting up, thumb poised on the hammer of his rifle, he listened. A moment later Lin Cooper's tones reached him, urgent, filled with alarm.

He rose instantly, and moving silently, walked down into the draw. Benson was standing over the girl who lay in the bed she'd prepared on the near side of the clearing.

"It's the way Nate said it was to be," Morg was saying. "You know that . . . Was always to be me and you."

Lin stirred. "I know, Morg. Only now I'm not sure."

"Why ain't you? We could have it real nice. We got all that money. We could get us a home, go into business . . . maybe a store. Hear they're needing stores real bad in Arizona."

"I don't know . . . We'll talk about it—"

"You knew before we run into Gault!" Benson snapped, abruptly angry. "Everything was fine 'til he come along. What's he been telling you?"

"Nothing. He hasn't once said anything."

"You're lying! You was up there with him last night two, maybe three, hours talking—and could be you was doing something else!"

"I was there because I couldn't sleep, wanted to talk," Lin said coldly.

"Could've talked to me."

"You were asleep—snoring."

"Well, you'd better get used to that because I ain't letting you back out on me now. We're going through with the whole works, just like we planned—the way Nate wanted."

"Nate was only—"

"And since we're getting married soon's we hit Lordsburg, I don't see no reason why we can't start being man and wife right now. Might sort've bring you back to your senses."

Benson dropped to his knees, hands clawing at the blanket in which Lin had wrapped herself. He jerked one corner loose. The girl screamed, flailed at him with both hands.

Before the cry had left her lips Frank Gault was across the clearing. He reached down, seized Morg Benson by the shoulder, spun him about. Morg cursed, grabbed for the pistol at his hip.

Gault swung his fist at the man's anger-contorted face, felt pain shoot up his arm as his knuckles connected with Benson's skull. The blow landed high on the head, failed even to stun him, served simply to knock him off balance. Cursing wildly, Morg struggled to draw his pistol, managed finally to clear it of the holster.

Frank lashed out with his foot, sent the weapon skittering off into the rocks. Then, calm, he stepped back, leveled his rifle at Benson.

"Ought to put a bullet through you," he said in a taut voice. "Would if I wasn't afraid of bringing the Apaches down on us."

Wheeling stiffly, he strode to where Benson's pistol lay, scooped it up, and jammed it into his waistband.

Looking back to Benson, he said: "Get up and crawl in under the rocks where you belong. You pull a stunt like that again and I'll kill you—Apaches or not!"

Benson glared at him in furious silence, began to draw himself upright. For a long minute he stood there as if gauging his chances, and then he turned around and made his way sullenly to his blanket.

Gault did not move until the man had settled down. When that was done, and without looking at the girl, he retraced his steps to the end of the draw. Anger was having its strong way with him, arousing the bitterness that came with being forced to change his own plans—all-important to him in this particular instance.

But he was stuck with it—stuck with both Lin Cooper and Morg Benson, and there wasn't anything he could do about it. One thing was for damned sure, however: he didn't have to put up with Morg's ways.

# 9

Lin Cooper, trembling beneath her thick woolen blanket, watched Morg Benson crawl into his bed and then Gault, in that peculiar stiff-kneed manner of his, stalk back to his place at the end of the wash.

For the first time in her life she had known complete and absolute fear, and the memory of Benson crouched over her, face glistening with sweat, eyes alight while his strong hands pulled at her was something she'd never be able to erase from her mind.

The full meaning of Nate's death was having its impact upon her now. Always before, she had depended upon him, looked to him for safety and for all else, taking for granted that everything would be all right and worrying not at all about anything.

All that had changed. No longer did she have him as father, mother, and strong brother—an all-powerful protector—to rely on. From the moment of his death a metamorphosis had taken place; she became fair game, vulnerable, a target for any man who took a fancy to her. And growing up in the shadow of Nate with no other woman around, she was at a loss as to how she might cope with such.

Morg seemed to think he had a claim on her, actually owned her, as one might own a piece of property. Being honest, she supposed there were some grounds for his assumption—the things Nate had said, the fact they'd been thrown together for several years while she was growing up in the Colorado hills.

But she'd never actually given Morg Benson any

real cause to believe he was more to her than just a friend—an older friend, in fact, who happened to be her brother's partner.

As for Nate and what he'd said about them, about Morg looking out for her, he had, as usual, been considering her welfare and best interests, but she did not think he meant they should become man and wife. He might have hoped for that, but only if she wanted it. Nate would not wish a union upon her if he thought she found it distasteful; he wanted only to be certain she would always be cared for, looked after, just as he had done ever since the war.

She wished Nate and Frank Gault had met sooner, that her brother could have come to know the man. He would have liked Frank. There was something about him that made you feel good, made you sure of things.

Lin felt a warmness run through her as she thought back over the past minutes. Gault had been a deadly figure standing there, so cool, so utterly efficient in his calmness . . . And his face . . . In the moonlight it had been a mask of suppressed fury, and she guessed that he had come within an inch of killing Morg—likely would have if she hadn't been present.

What would it be like married to him? Most of the time he was so quiet, so withdrawn, almost to the point of shyness. And courteous—he treated her as if she were some grand lady, like the ones she saw on the pages of *Godey's Magazine,* a publication that Nate used to bring her now and then. She suspected Frank Gault treated all women that way, and thinking it over, she decided she liked him for it.

Was he already married? Did he have a girl somewhere whom he intended to make his wife one day?

She wondered about that, recalled that he'd never mentioned or given the slightest hint of it. Staring into the sky, she doubted the possibility. Frank Gault was not the sort who'd go galavanting around the land if he had a wife. Either he'd stay with her, or he'd take her wherever he went. He'd be that kind.

Tomorrow she'd try to learn more about him . . . Tomorrow she'd manage to somehow weasel it out of him, discover whether he was married or pledged to become so. One thing was certain. She was finished with Morg Benson once and for all. When they got to Lordsburg she'd give him his half of the money, and they'd go their separate ways. If she never saw him again after that, it would be too soon.

As to her own future, she'd decide that in Lordsburg, too. A lot—in fact just about everything—depended on what she learned from Frank Gault about himself tomorrow. If he were already married, that ended it . . . but if not—well, she guessed a man could be considered fair game the same as a woman.

Benson sprawled on his blankets, not bothering to draw the covering over his body, and watched the fleeting clouds drift through the night sky. There was still a ringing in his head from the blow he'd taken from Frank Gault just as there had been no diminishing of the anger and hate that had sprung alive within him.

Goddam him! Maybe he'd won the first round, but this was only the beginning! If Gault thought he had everything sliding his way, he'd better guess again. Nobody had ever pushed Morg Benson around and gotten away with it. Always the day had come when, one way or another, he'd evened the score.

And this, for sure, was one time when that was going to hold true.

Lin Cooper was his, rightfully so, and no two-bit saddle tramp was going to take her away from him— not while he was still breathing! He'd had his eye on her ever since he and Nate Cooper had teamed up.

He'd watched her turn from a gangling kid with stringy hair into a well-curved woman fit to stir a man to fire, and he'd just waited for the day when he could claim her. That he was twelve, maybe fourteen, years older counted for nothing. Hell, he was a lot more man than she'd ever be able to take care of! Anyway, it was better that way—the husband being older than the wife. It made for a lot less trouble.

Women got funny ideas, like the way Lin was being taken in by this Gault, and it required a firm hand to straighten them out when they sort of got out of line. That's what Lin needed—straightening out, and he was just the man jack to do it.

And there was the money . . . They had twenty thousand good old United States dollars between them, more or less. A pile of cash! Man could do plenty with that much, set himself up in great style.

But sure as hell not out here in this God-forsaken land of sand and heat and bloodthirsty savages. New Orleans—that was the place for a man with money jingling in his pockets. Plenty of opportunity there in the importing business, he'd heard. Buying and selling stuff from Cuba and the West Indies. Fortunes could be made overnight.

But first things first.

Everything he'd worked and schemed for insofar as Lin was concerned was in danger of upset because of Frank Gault. And if he lost her, he lost also the ten thousand dollars he would naturally acquire when she became his wife. Smart thing to do was step right in and eliminate that danger.

On top of that there was the little matter of this Gault slapping him around. That came under the heading of personal satisfaction, and he'd have it before the last bell rang. Hell, they didn't need Gault. It wasn't even necessary they go on to Lordsburg. Cut east through the mountains. Sure to be a town over there somewhere.

Morg Benson, muscles quivering expectantly, devious mind working smoothly, sat up. A hard grin was on his lips. That was it. Get rid of Gault, head east. That was the right direction to go if he wanted to reach New Orleans.

He glanced to Lin. She was awake, staring at the stars, mooning over that goddamned Gault, most likely. Come tomorrow night he'd give her something else to think about . . . He wished she'd go to sleep. Then he could go about his business.

## 10

Gault made himself as comfortable as possible on the knoll, laid his rifle across his knees, and rubbed at his skinned knuckles ruefully. Morg Benson's head was hard as flint.

He glanced to the north, located the red flare of the outlaw's campfire, grunted. Still there . . . Fools to build such a blaze . . . Apaches five miles off would have it pinpointed. That was good, far as he was concerned. It would keep wandering braves thinking about that end of the mountain.

He sighed gustily, again thought how good it would be to reach Lordsburg, rid himself of Lin Cooper and Benson . . . Damn it all—he'd bargained for none of it, particularly for the job of protecting the girl from her overanxious husband-to-be.

Or was that how it was? From the way it looked now, and recalling what Lin had said, it would appear the idea was all Morg's, and she was having nothing to do with the plans he had in mind.

Regardless, it was their business and they could straighten it out to suit themselves once they got to the settlement. All he was interested in was delivering them safely and heading on for Tucson where, hopefully, Jud Weatherby would still be waiting for him. If he'd been running in any luck at all, he'd not gotten mixed up with the Cooper party in the first place, but there were times when things just dropped into a man's lap and he had no choice except to make the best of it.

It wouldn't be his problem for much longer. A couple of days, if everything went well. All he need do was hold the outlaws at a respectable distance, keep his eyes peeled for Apaches, and bear southeast until he touched the lower tip of the Burro Mountains. Then, once out of White Rock Canyon and on the plains, Lordsburg would be in sight.

He hoped he'd have no more trouble with Benson and wondered idly why the man's attentions toward the girl had riled him so. It was natural to stop the man in what he was trying to do simply because of Lin's objections, but to get so worked up personally over it didn't make sense.

Well, it had happened, and regardless of what it was that prompted him to such heat, it was neither here nor there. Things would go all right if Benson kept his distance and left the girl alone. If he didn't, he'd damned quick find himself tied hand and foot to a saddle; there were too many critical things to worry about.

Somewhere back on the mountain a lion screamed into the hush. Gault cocked an ear toward the horses, wondered if the big cat had caught wind of them and was endeavoring to move in for a kill. The horses appeared to be undisturbed and he guessed there was no danger. He'd have a look around later, just to be sure, however.

The outlaws' fire seemed to be brighter. They were really asking for trouble . . . Greenhorns, no doubt. No man of experience would tempt luck in Apache country with such a conflagration. Of course, there were five of them, and numbers evidently were giving them confidence. That was sheer stupidity. Apaches didn't always run in small parties; he'd seen as many as twenty, even thirty, in a bunch.

The solid thud of heels brought him around, rifle coming up swiftly and without conscious thought.

"Only me," Morg Benson said hastily, raising his hands and moving in slowly.

Gault relented, studied the husky man narrowly and with distaste.

"Couldn't sleep. Figured I ought to take the time, tell you I'm right sorry about the way I acted back there."

Frank Gault shrugged, caring not at all.

"Want you to know I ain't holding no hard feelings. Expect I did sort of get out of line. You was right to stop me."

"Forget it. Just don't let it happen again."

"It won't. Got my word on that. Was only—well, me and Lin's aiming to marry up and I couldn't see no reason why we shouldn't go ahead being man and wife now. You understand that, I guess."

Gault's shoulders stirred. "Sounds to me like she's got other ideas about marrying you."

Benson squatted on his heels beside Gault, scooped up a handful of sand, began to toy with it, spilling it back and forth from one cupped palm to the other.

"Crazy notion she's just took on. Be a different story, come morning. Nate always said—"

"Nate's dead. She's doing her own thinking now."

Anger showed on Benson's face. "You trying to say she's gone sweet on you?"

"Me?" Frank said and laughed. "Hell, no! I'm just telling you she's not thinking about you. Got other plans, once we're in Lordsburg."

"That'll change, like I said. Been waiting for her to grow up six, seven, years. She's my woman—"

"Along with her share of the twenty thousand dollars—"

"Only part of it," Benson said mildly. "Ain't saying all that money don't make it real nice, but far as it being the main thing, it ain't so. Just that us getting married's been all cut and dried for a long time . . . Want you to understand that."

"Means nothing to me," Gault said bluntly, "but

don't force the issue while I'm around. Once we get to Lordsburg, you're on your own—both of you. She'll have the law to look out for her if she's decided she wants nothing to do with you."

"Ain't the way it'll be," Morg said doggedly. "You'll see. I know that girl, maybe better'n she knows herself." He paused, stared off into the north. "That the bunch that's following us?"

"On the same trail we took—and no Apache would build a bonfire like that."

Benson reached for additional sand, glanced over his shoulder. "You really figure there's Indians hanging around here? Sure ain't no sign."

"Won't see any, or hear anything, either. But they're around—or will be. That fire'll tip them off that there're whites on the trail."

"Long as it draws them down there won't be nothing for us to worry about."

Gault gave no answer. The conversation bored him, and he was feeling the need for a little sleep. He wished Benson would return to his blankets. There'd been no more indication of the lion's presence, and he guessed the cat had just been prowling through the area.

"What's east of here?"

"Fifty miles of mountains," he said wearily.

"Any towns?"

"Couple—Pinos Altos, Silver City. Mining settlements."

"Can you get to them from here?"

"Be hard going. No trail."

Morg nodded. "Can see why you're taking us to Lordsburg."

"Happened to be the way I was headed."

"But a man could get through—east, I mean, was he of a mind?"

Frank nodded. "He could. You thinking about changing your mind, taking off on your own?"

"Me? Not much. Just asking, that's all. You're bossing this shindig. We'll do it your way."

Benson rose to his feet, yawned. "Well, reckon I'd best turn in. Expect you're figuring on an early start."

"By daylight."

Morg bobbed his head. "Good. I'll be ready," he said, and then wheeling swiftly, flung the sand he palmed straight into Gault's eyes.

Blinded, Frank staggered to his feet. He felt the rifle being torn from his grasp, heard Morg Benson's harsh voice.

"Goddam you—I'll teach you to go sticking your nose in where it don't belong!"

Clawing at his eyes, Gault tried to move away. He tripped, went to his knees. In the next instant something crashed into the back of his head and a world of hushed darkness engulfed him.

# 11

Benson, mouth working convulsively, sweat clothing his face, stared down at Frank Gault's limp figure.

"Lousy saddle bum!" he snarled in a wild voice. "Reckon you know now who you're fooling with!"

Drawing back his foot, he drove a booted toe into the unconscious man's ribs, laughed shrilly as Gault's reflexes responded automatically.

Shifting the rifle to his left hand, he seized Gault by the arm, turned, dragged him into the wash. Leaving him in a heap near the dead campfire, he crossed to where the girl lay.

"Lin!" he shouted, ripping the blanket off her. "Get up! Want you to look at your big man now!"

Lin Cooper, startled from a sound sleep, senses

drugged, eyes wide with fright, struggled to her feet. Benson reached out, grabbed the wealth of thick hair on the back of her head, forced her to face Gault.

"See—he ain't so goddammed much!"

The girl's hand flew to her lips, stifling a cry. She took a step toward the unconscious man. Savagely, Benson jerked her back, spun her away.

"No, you don't!" he yelled. "From now on I'm running things. You're paying mind to me, hear?"

Lin tried to draw back, but he held tight to her hair. "You're—you're crazy—"

He laughed again. "Yeh, like a fox. Just looking out for myself—and what's mine."

The girl was calming, the shock of the first stunning moments having passed. She studied him covertly, and then subtlety narrowed her eyes.

"Sure, Morg. But what're we going to do?"

His brows lifted in surprise. He grinned, released his hold upon her. "Now you're showing some sense," he said. "We're getting out of here, that's what we're doing. Just you 'n' me . . . Pass me that hunk of rope laying there behind you."

Lin remained motionless, considering his words and intentions. Sudden temper distorted Benson's face again. He raised his hand threateningly, prepared to strike her. Lin recoiled, picked up the length of rope used to bind her blanket roll, tossed it to him.

He caught it, squatted beside Gault. Crossing the man's wrists behind him, Morg lashed them together. With the surplus length of the rope he bound the ankles.

Lin watched in a sort of stupefied silence while horror mounted steadily within her.

"He'll—die!" she said in a strangled voice.

Benson drew himself upright, grinned at her. "Maybe some of them 'Paches he keeps talking about'll come along, hurry things up a mite."

Lin shuddered. Morg seemed out of his mind completely. She tried to make some sense of it, understand what had happened to bring it about, concluded it stemmed wholly from the incident earlier that night. She looked at him intently, seeing a Morg Benson she never knew existed.

"There's no need to kill him," she said, fighting to keep her voice level.

Benson spat, drove another brutal toe into Gault's ribs. "Hell there ain't."

"Why?"

"For fooling with me, that's why. Getting in my way—and filling you with all kinds of notions. I ain't standing for none of it!"

"But to kill him—"

"Know his kind. If'n I don't, he'll be dogging my heels from here on."

"Because of me . . ."

Benson spat again. "Reckon that's it, mostly. You been talking and acting up, saying you was going to do things, and he was egging you on. Expect what he was planning was to get rid of me, take you with him."

"That's wrong, Morg. It's not true—any of it."

The squat man shook his head. "I got eyes and ears. I know what was going on."

"You just thought it was that way." Lin's tone had assumed a thread of desperation. "He never gave me a second thought, except as a job he had to do . . . It's wrong to kill him for something he—"

"Know what I seen," Benson said stubbornly, his bloodshot eyes on Gault.

"Whatever it was, you misunderstood . . . Let him go, Morg, and I'll do whatever you want. Don't leave him here to die."

"You're doing what I tell you, anyway," Benson said with a malevolent grin. "Go get the horses. We're pulling out."

Lin remained rooted to the spot. "I won't let you do this," she declared firmly, thrusting her hands into the pockets of her riding skirt. "I refuse to help. You'll have to make me."

"Can do that, too," Benson said blandly, and seizing her by the arm, slapped her hard across the face.

The force of the blow staggered her, sent her stumbling toward the upper end of the wash where Gault had picketed the horses.

"Now you bring them goddammed animals down here like I told you!" he shouted after her. "Keep on getting cute with me and I'll make you wish you'd never been born!"

Dazed, Lin collected her scattered wits. Hope was soaring through her, blotting out the pain the blow had caused, however. Her fingers had touched the cool metal of the clasp knife in her pocket. Once it had been Nate's but he had long ago given it to her, and she had formed the habit of carrying it with her, finding it handy in performing her chores around the cabin. It was small, but the blades were sharp.

Moving on, she reached the horses, began to pull at the pickets. Seizing the opportunity while her back was to the camp, she produced the knife, opened the largest blade, and slipped it inside her shirt. Quickly then she completed her task.

In the clearing Benson was dragging gear from the brush where Frank Gault had hidden it. "Get your horses saddled," he ordered, picking up his own hull. "Don't be all morning about it."

Silent, Lin went about the job of making ready the bay. Benson, finishing before she, immediately started throwing tack on Gault's horse.

Dismay flooded Lin. "You taking him, too?"

"Taking 'em all," Morg said. "Never know when one of the others'll go lame." He paused, fixed her with a suspicious stare. "You tricking me or something?"

"No," she replied hastily. "Wondered why you were bothering with an extra horse, that's all."

Benson continued to glare as if not sure he could believe her. Lin ignored him, turned, began to saddle Nate's black. She had made a bad slip, almost given herself away.

"Are we going on to Lordsburg?" she asked, frantically trying to channel his thoughts to a different direction.

It worked. Lin breathed deeper, hearing him resume his work with Gault's buckskin.

"Nope," he said. "Changed my mind."

"Then, where—"

"Heading east, over the mountains. Couple of towns over there where we can catch up a stagecoach and light out for New Orleans."

Lin rocked with surprise. "New Orleans!" she echoed in amazement. "Thought we were going to Arizona!"

"Small pickings. Been thinking about New Orleans for a long time. Can take the twenty thousand, turn it into ten times that much buying and selling on the islands."

Gault was stirring feebly, struggling to regain consciousness. Benson, facing the other way, did not notice. Lin felt a new flow of anxiety rush through her. If Frank roused, Morg likely would kill him where he lay. Immediately she began to hurry her movements, hasten to get the saddling of the black finished.

"Guess we're ready," Benson said suddenly, moving to her side. "You sure you got everything cinched tight? Don't want nothing slipping while we're climbing through them mountains."

"Tight as I could pull," the girl said, recognizing the moment she'd prayed for. "Maybe you ought to test the buckles, be certain."

"Yeh, maybe I ought," Morg agreed, and reached for the black's cinch strap.

Lin backed a few steps, hand going swiftly inside her shirt for the knife. She'd have that one chance, no more.

Gripping the small weapon firmly in her palm, she took another backward stride, felt her heel come up against Gault's body. Immediately she released her fingers. The knife fell upon his shoulder, clung momentarily, and slid to the ground at his side.

Breathing easier, pulse quieting, she returned to where her horse stood, swung onto the saddle. Benson grinned at her.

"Seems you're kind of anxious to get moving. Figured you would be once you seen how things was."

Lin, hoping to keep his mind off Frank Gault and a possible final look by Morg that could result in the discovery of the knife, nodded.

"Thinking about those outlaws. They'll be coming soon. If we're ever to get to New Orleans we don't want them following us."

Benson clucked approvingly at that bit of wisdom, glanced toward the north. "About forgot them."

"They've not forgotten us. I'm sure of that."

"Can bet on it," he agreed, and stepped to his saddle. "Best we get out of here fast as we can."

Settling himself, he threw his attention to Gault. A frown pulled at his features. Lin felt her heart skip a beat.

"Rap I give him sure must've cooled him good."

"Probably be unconscious for hours," Lin commented, grasping at smoke wisps. "I don't think you realize how strong you are." The words almost gagged her but they had to be said.

Morg Benson leered at her happily. Jamming Gault's rifle into the boot, he leaned forward, winked broadly.

"Girl, you plain don't know how much man you're getting!" he said, swinging around and taking up the reins of Nate's horse. "First chance we get we'll make camp and I'll show you . . . Come on, grab a hold of them leathers and let's get moving."

A combination of fear and relief flooded through Lin Cooper: a fear for what lay ahead for her, relief that Frank Gault would have his chance to survive.

Kneeing her bay in close, she gathered up the buckskin's reins and followed Morg Benson out of the wash.

## 12

Frank Gault opened his eyes. All was silent around him, and the pale flare in the sky told him the night was almost gone. Unsure, he lay motionless, conscious of a sickening pulse of pain in his head and side, aware that his hands and ankles were bound tightly. Without moving his head he could see that he was in the wash where camp had been made. Whether he was alone or not was an uncertainty.

His fogged brain began to struggle for comprehension. It was an effort to think, to concentrate, and there were gaps in his memory . . . He'd been sitting at the edge of the clearing. Benson had come up. They'd talked. And then Benson had thrown sand into his eyes. He'd jumped up, tried to defend himself, but unable to see, he'd tripped, fallen. Right after that he'd been struck from behind, had blacked out. Undoubtedly Morg was responsible for that, too.

The next thing he remembered was the sound of voices, fading in and out, seemingly coming from a great distance. Who had been speaking he could not recall, perhaps did not even know at the time, as all things were in a state of wavering obscurity. And that, too, had later slid down into a thick mist.

His mind was clearing. The crisp bite of the early morning air was reviving him, melting the fog, restoring some degree of strength to his body. The pain in his head was increasing also, as was the dull ache in his side, but he was functioning, beginning to think straight.

One thing was clear: trussed up tight he was in a bad way, although possibly in no immediate danger.

Raising his head slightly to verify that, he looked around the wash, gray-shadowed with first light. It was deserted. His eyes shifted to the pocket of brush where he had cached the gear . . . Nothing. He could not see the upper area where he had tethered the horses, but he knew without looking they would be missing also.

Anger gripped him. He sank back, swearing in a harsh, frustrated way. Benson had played him for a sucker, had tricked him neatly and then pulled out, leaving him to die—either by thirst and starvation or at the hands of marauding Apaches. Rolling over, he sat up, swore again, cursing the moment he'd encountered Morg Benson and the Coopers, the ill luck that had brought them together.

Why the hell did it have to be him? Why didn't he turn his back on them right at the start, keep out of it, and let them face their own problems? Now, because of that sonofabitch of a Benson, who seemed to think he was after the girl, he was lying hog-tied out in the middle of nowhere with nothing ahead but death.

"Pigheaded, locoed fool!" he muttered, struggling against the ropes that bound his wrists. "Damn him to hell!"

The cords only cut deeper into his arms. He lay back, resting on one elbow, sweat streaming from his face, despite the coolness. His eyes halted on the fire. It appeared dead, but there might be a coal or two with a spark of life. If he could find one, blow it into a flame, burn through the rope . . .

He twisted about, began to hitch his way laboriously toward the mound of gray ashes. The hard glitter of metal at his side caught his attention. His jaw sagged . . . A knife . . . one blade open.

Gault stared at the small weapon unbelievingly, and then it came to him: Lin had placed it there. Somehow, without Morg Benson seeing her, she had managed to leave it for him.

Coming entirely around, he probed blindly in the dirt with his fingers until he located the knife and took a firm grip on it. Drawing himself to his knees, legs doubled beneath him, he slashed at the cords that bound his ankles until they parted.

He felt better. Rising, he hurried into the shelter of the brush. It would take time to maneuver around to where he could work on the rope holding his wrists together—and someone could come along, catch him there, helpless. Best to hide, take no chances.

It required less time than he anticipated. The knife blade was razor sharp, and after he'd managed to get it into an effective position, nicking himself twice in the process, he found the strands of the rope parted readily under the edge of the blade.

Free, he stood in the undergrowth chafing his wrists, relieving the tingle that restored blood-circulation was causing while his eyes searched the wash patiently. It appeared Morg Benson had left nothing behind. His rifle . . . He recalled he'd been struck down at the edge of the wash. Benson had wrenched it from his grasp, used it as a club. Perhaps Morg had dropped it, let it lie.

Pausing a moment to listen, scan the surrounding brush for signs of others nearby, he stepped into the open, trotted to the end of the arroyo. Pain stabbed at his ribs, and his head felt as if it were going to fall from his shoulders, but he ignored it all, reached the mound where he had sat. Disappointment slogged through him.

The carbine was not there, only a brushed-looking trail bordered by twin grooves made by his boot heels when Benson had dragged him down into the clearing. He gave that thought; why had Morg gone to all that extra work? The answer was simple, came quickly; to show off before Lin, prove to her what a big man he was. Morg Benson's mind functioned at that level.

That could be the only reason, and it indicated more: Benson was feeling sure of himself. He'd be taking his time, confident he'd seen the last of the man he figured was at the bottom of his troubles. Therefore, he would not be far ahead. A couple of hours, perhaps three. And if his thoughts pertaining to Lin yet flowed in the same low channel as they had earlier, he'd be looking for a place to stop, make camp.

Moving slowly, lost in consideration, Gault made his way to the upper end of the wash where he'd picketed the horses. All were gone, as he had expected, but he had to be sure.

That was the end of it. His connection with the Cooper party was finished. That Lin had not gone with Benson willingly was certain, but that could hardly be listed as any concern of his. Whatever was between them had begun long before he had entered the picture.

Forget them all; dismiss them from his mind then and there—Lin, Morg Benson, and their twenty-thousand-dollar stake, the outlaws, the whole kit—and worry about his own serious predicament. Unarmed and on foot, he'd be a fool to follow.

Only smart thing for him to do was strike out across the hills for Lordsburg and hope he could make it. He'd have his hands full trying to get there avoiding Apaches and living off the land with only a pocket knife as a weapon.

The knife...

He stared at it, frowned. Lin, at undoubtedly great risk, had placed it there for him to find. She wanted to be sure he'd escape the death Morg Benson had planned for him—just as surely as she hoped he'd follow, rescue her from Benson.

Gault swore, that disturbing thought having its way with him. Could he ignore her obvious appeal for help? Could he head out for Lordsburg knowing that somewhere she was waiting and praying for him to come?

Perhaps it wasn't that way at all . . . Very possibly she left the knife out of pity, wanted only to provide him with a means of escape . . . That was it.

But Frank Gault couldn't convince himself. He kept

remembering the revulsion on her face, the terror in her eyes that night before when Morg had crouched over her as she lay in her blankets. That hadn't been the look of a woman ready to take a man as husband; it had been a portrayal of sheer horror.

He couldn't do it, couldn't ignore her. He'd forget going on to Lordsburg, stick instead to the more roundabout trail they had been following, and attempt to overtake them. If, as he suspected, Benson was moving leisurely, chances were good he could catch up soon if he moved right along.

The outlaws . . .

They came to mind in that next instant. He could expect them to be on the move. They'd been a considerable distance behind, but riding, it wouldn't take them long to overcome the lead. Be smart to wipe out the trail left by Lin and Benson, confuse the five men as much as possible. Such would cost a few precious minutes but it would prove worth it.

Wheeling, he cut a fair-sized branch off a clump of rabbit brush, trotted out of the wash to the trail. The tracks where they had entered that night before were plain. He left them undisturbed, moved farther over, began to search for the prints that would have been made by the departure.

He found none. Mystified, he hunted about for several minutes, then paused, a scrap of the conversation he'd had with Benson coming to mind. Doubling back, he made his way to the head of the clearing.

There he picked up the hoof prints made when the horses had been led from the brush. He found where they had stood while being saddled and bridled—and he discovered where, in single file, they had moved out of the wash and pointed due east into the heart of the mountains.

"The fool!" Gault muttered. "The damned fool!"

There'd be no trail for them to follow; only mile after endless mile of dense forest, thick brush, steep, rock-covered slopes, buttes, and bottomless canyons.

Even the most experienced would think twice before tackling such a trip.

It would be slow going. Frank smiled with grim satisfaction at that thought. It would take less time than he had figured to catch up. A man on foot could cover ground much faster than one riding and leading a string of horses.

Using the length of brush as a broom, he turned to the file of hoof prints leading from the wash, swept them smooth, and sprinkled dust over the freshly turned earth. When he reached the thick brush, he threw the branch into a bramble where it would not be noticed. There was no further need to hide the trail; it was lost already in the rocks and leaves that littered the ground.

Glancing to the sky, now shot with streaks of orange and yellow, he moved off at a slow trot, eyes reaching ahead. He'd have to follow as best he could, guided by an occasional broken branch, an overturned stone, an isolated hoof mark. But it wouldn't be too difficult. Benson, traveling blind, would simply head east, turning aside only when barriers the horses could not surmount blocked his path.

Frank Gault came to a sudden stop. Directly ahead, blocking his way, were three Apaches.

# 13

Lin Cooper allowed herself to slump on the saddle, rock with the motion of her horse. She was cold but it was not entirely from the keenness of the light breeze fanning across the hills; it came also from her thoughts of what lay ahead.

Her gaze settled on Benson a short distance in front of her. He was a thick shape on his horse, bull neck almost lost in his hunched shoulders. She trembled, half turned, cast a hopeful glance to the rear. There was no sign of Frank Gault.

Surely he had regained consciousness by then and found the knife. It had been more than an hour since Morg Benson had led her out of the wash. He should be free of his bonds and, she prayed, trailing them.

But there was no real assurance. He could have been seriously injured, even fatally, by the blow Morg had given him. And those kicks—enough to break a man's ribs. Besides, there were the Apaches to think of. They could have come, found him helpless, killed him where he lay. The same applied to the outlaws. Knowing he had helped her, along with Nate and Morg, they'd show him no mercy, either.

A shiver passed through her again, and then a different trend of thought claimed her mind. Frank Gault would be all right. He was one of those who could take care of himself, meet any emergency however dire, overcome it. No need to worry about him. Frank would be all right.

And he would come.

She wished there had been some way she could leave a marked trail for him to follow. Morg was cutting across country, sticking to no path since there actually wasn't one to follow. If only she'd been able to leave scraps of cloth, bits of paper—anything. But she brushed that aside also as of no importance. Frank could track them. He'd spot the point of their passage quickly, stay on it as easily as if it were a boardwalk. He had that sort of ability.

She should help, however, do what she could to make it simpler, faster for him . . . Create a delay, that was it. Slow Benson down. She'd watch her chances, grab the first opportunity.

She could expect to pay for such an incident, and it wouldn't be pleasant. Her head still ached, and a soreness had developed along her cheekbone where Morg had slapped her. It would be worth it, just the same. Anything that would help Frank Gault would justify the penalty.

*What if he doesn't come?*

The small, suppressed voice of doubt within her finally made itself heard. What if he decided it was no affair of his, that she was not his worry, and free of the ropes that bound him, continued on to Lordsburg? He had no real reason to help her—none—except that he was a decent man.

Thin reasoning . . . Why should he deliberately mix himself into her troubles? Theirs had been nothing more than a chance encounter, an accident that threw them together for a brief time, and he had emerged the worse for it.

She couldn't blame him if he washed his hands of the whole mess, continued on his way. Why should he further endanger his life trying to help her? While she had found him attractive and more than just interesting, he'd shown no particular regard for her. He'd treated her just as he would any other woman, probably . . . Maybe she was a fool to hope—to look for him.

*He'll come . . . He'll come.*

The greater strength of another voice within Lin Cooper pushed to the fore, made itself known, calming her fears and doubts that threatened to hurl her into panic. She didn't know why, and all logic denied the possibility, but she was convinced Frank Gault would come.

It was full light. The sun, still behind the towering ridges and peaks before them, was up and well on its way into the heavens. A warmness had begun to spread through the clean, clear air, and the land seemed to have come alive. Small animals darted in and out of the brush, birds flitted through the densely growing trees, and momentarily the throttling fear she had of Morg Benson faded.

But that recess from horror ended abruptly. She saw him twist his squat torso, grin back at her.

"Everything fine, hon?"

She nodded woodenly, features frozen.

"Be pulling up soon. Can fix us some vittles and do a spell of resting. Expect you're tired. Been looking for a good spot."

The dread Lin had so carefully avoided dwelling upon from the moment they'd ridden out of the arroyo, broke its bounds in that instant. Soaring fear seized her, and as Benson swung his flushed face back to the front, she glanced frantically around. A narrow aisle between the tall pines opened to her left.

Immediately she released her grip upon the reins of the horse she led, and digging heels into the bay, whirled from the line and raced off into the dappled shadows.

She heard Benson shout a startled, angry oath. The fear within her surged to greater heights. From the tail of her eye she saw Morg wheel, come plunging down the lane in pursuit. Crouched low, she cried to her horse for more speed.

It was hopeless. Benson was upon her, rushing in alongside, almost, it seemed, before she had really gotten started.

He leaned over, snatched the bay's reins from her hands, hauled to a stop. Lin sagged weakly in the saddle, sobbing helplessly. She scarcely noticed when he dropped from his mount, strode to her side.

"So that's how it's to be!" he snarled, seizing her arm in a crushing grip. "Can't be trusted atall! All right, I'll just fix things good!"

Walking ahead, he led the horses back to where the others had stopped. Pausing beside his own mount, he pulled a length of rawhide from his saddlebags.

"You're wanting me to be mean. Good enough, I'll

be mean," he said, voice trembling with anger. "Stick out your hands."

Obediently Lin extended her arms. Crossing her wrists, he lashed them together with the leather string, affixed the trailing end to the horn of her saddle.

"Reckon that'll make you behave," Morg said, stepping back. "And it ain't coming off—not 'til you come begging. Understand?"

Lin stared at him. He hadn't struck her as she'd expected, and somehow that seemed, in some obscure way, a victory. Courage lifted within her.

"I'll never beg—never!" she said defiantly.

He grinned, exposing his broad teeth. "Sure you will. You'll be begging before the day's over. Wait and see."

Reaching back, he took the reins of the horse she'd been leading, tied them to a ring on the skirt of her saddle. Taking them, the bay's leathers, he attached them in the same manner to the horse he was leading. He nodded to her.

"Kind of like the old days in Colorado . . . Got me a regular pack train."

Lin made no reply. He studied her silently for a long minute, shrugged when she said nothing, and walked to his horse. Halting abruptly, he retraced his steps.

"Been aiming to do this," he said.

Jerking the straps free, he removed the bags containing the money from her saddle. Slinging it over his shoulder, he added: "I'll do the looking after it from now on. Be better that way. Never did figure it was safe with you."

A glimmer of hope came to her. "Take it all. You can have my share if you'll let me go."

He hesitated once more to stare at her from his small, red-rimmed eyes.

"You won't even have to take me back. I'll take my chances, find the trail somehow . . . Just let me go."

Benson's lips split into an unpleasant grin. "Still mooning over Gault, eh? Forget him. Dead now."

"Maybe not. If I hurried—"

"And far as me turning you loose for your share of the money, that'd be downright foolish of me, now wouldn't it? I already got the money, and I got you, too . . . Something I've always hankered for—a lot of money and a pretty woman. Sure don't aim to give either one up now."

## 14

The Apaches had been waiting for him. They'd heard him coming from the distance, simply drew their lean little ponies to a stop, bided their time, and let him blunder straight into them. Rigid, Frank Gault watched them coolly.

Young bucks out to blood themselves—and provide themselves with weapons. One had only a rifle, an old, single-shot army gun taken no doubt from some luckless cavalryman. His two companions each carried an ax and a feathered lance. Their faces were paint-streaked, and in the rising sunlight their near-naked bodies gleamed like soft copper. As did most Indians, they rode bareback, scorning saddles in the belief that they added unnecessary weight to their mounts.

They appeared surprised, angry that he was unarmed. The one with the rifle said something in quick Spanish. The others yelled, and abruptly the youngest of the trio raised his arm, hurled his lance. Frank leaped to one side. The spear point drove into the soft loam, leaving the shaft upright. Gault wrenched the quivering weapon free, lunged into the nearby brush.

Instantly more yells went up. All three braves charged, bearing down on Gault in a pounding of hooves. He whirled, hearing one immediately at his heels . . . the one with the rifle. The Apache aimed, jerked at the trigger. The gun roared and the heavy slug thudded into a tree stump yards wide of its target.

The brave, mouth blared open in a piercing screech, swept in, endeavored to bring the rifle around, use it as a club. Gault ducked to the side, caught at the thick stock of the weapon, threw his weight against it. The Apache slipped to one side of his plunging horse, started to fall. He released his grasp on the carbine, clutched at the horse's mane, rushed on.

Yells were ricocheting around Frank Gault in a continuing din. He threw the useless carbine into the brush, spun to meet the others, now swinging back in upon him. The young brave deserted his pony, was racing in, ax poised. Gault scooped up the lance he'd dropped, wedged its end against his instep, and met the Apache's rush with the wickedly sharp point of the weapon.

The young buck skewered himself on the blade, threw up his arms, and screamed. The shaft of the lance bowed under his weight, snapped.

Moving fast, Gault ducked into the brush. His one hope was motion, offer no target for the remaining brave who still possessed both ax and lance. He didn't know what had happened to the one who'd carried the rifle. Unarmed now, he would likely stay out of it unless he saw an opportunity to use the knife he undoubtedly carried.

An instant later Gault heard again the quick hammer of hooves. Movement flickered in the brush on either side. The two were trying to pocket him, trap him between their horses. They'd have him then, pinned down, unable to turn.

He stopped short, dropped low, wheeled. Something whirred over his head, clanked against the tree beyond him . . . An ax. Desperate, he grabbed up the weapon, pivoted again. He could hear the brush crackling at his heels, knew one of the braves was almost upon him intent now in riding him down. He took a long step aside, swung the ax with all his strength—his target the head of the Apache's horse. The rusty blade drove deep into the animal's skull between the wildly rolling eyes. The horse dropped in his tracks.

The brave yelled, launched himself at Frank as the horse caved in under him. Gault, off balance, fell backward, but his upstretched hands caught the slim, sweaty body of the Apache, propelled him head on into the thick trunk of the pine behind him.

The sound of the Indian's yell died abruptly as his head smashed into the tree and his body collapsed in a heap at its base.

Gasping for breath, sweat-soaked, his muscles crying for rest, Frank Gault picked himself up, looked for the third brave. There was no sign of him. He groaned in relief, sagged against a stump. That he possessed strength enough to match another enemy bent on taking his life he had strong doubts.

After a moment he mopped at his face, stared down at the Apache. He was dead like the one impaled on the lance; what he looked for, hopefully, was a weapon that could be of use to him. Apaches cared little for handguns, preferring rifles above all else, but occasionally one did carry a pistol which he kept hidden in the folds of his cotton drawers or breechcloth. Since these were all young braves they likely owned nothing except the weapons he'd seen, but he had to be sure.

Nothing . . . Sighing, Gault examined the other Apache, came up with the same result. He turned to the dead horse, wrenched the ax free. It wasn't much with which to protect himself, but it was better than no weapon at all. He moved on after that, eyes alert for the third brave. Seemingly, he had disappeared completely, fading off into the brush wanting no more of the fight.

But he would return, Gault realized grimly. He'd round up a few more of his kind and they'd all be back, armed and seeking vengeance. He'd be something special to them now—a white man who'd slain two of their number in hand-to-hand combat. It would mean big medicine for the brave who brought him down.

They'd have to find him first. He glanced around, searching for the horse of the buck he'd pinned with the lance, caught sight of him standing among the trees near where his rider had died. Dropping low, Frank doubled back through the clumps of mountain mahogany and oak, approached the pony from the rear. Within only paces the horse caught wind of him, and hating the white-man smell, threw back his head and galloped off into the trees.

Gault swore, straightened up. He could have made good use of the pony, but as well forget him; the horse wouldn't let him get nearer than fifty yards now.

Thrusting the short handle of the ax under his belt, he moved to where he had last noted tracks left by Benson and Lin Cooper. Locating them, he resumed the pursuit, moving quietly and fairly fast. He had no idea of the direction the escaping Apache had taken and knew he must necessarily watch sharp. He had encountered the trio as he was moving east; that could mean others would be in the same general area.

It could also mean that Benson and the girl had ridden into an Apache party and been captured. His jaw hardened as he considered that possibility. What Apaches did to white women wasn't pretty.

If only he had a gun—a weapon that would equalize the odds somewhat should he come upon another band of braves. The old army carbine would have been better than nothing, but he'd had no cartridges for it. The Apache he'd taken it from was the one who had disappeared during the fight. If he possessed extra ammunition, it had gone with him.

He pressed on steadily, eyes and ears keened for

motion or sound foreign to the usual noises and movements of the country around him. The sun had climbed higher and he began to thirst, but he was deep in a part of the hills that were not familiar to him. He'd made the trip east across the mountains once before, but the course he'd followed lay farther north.

His pace began to lag, his breath to come with greater effort. Finally he pulled down to a walk, now swinging his eyes back and forth continually as he sought the lush growth that would indicate a spring or a small stream. There would be water somewhere. It had been a wet season; even the smallest creeks would be flowing.

He found none. Either they were above or below him, and he was reluctant, despite his burning thirst, to abandon the erratic trail Benson was leaving in his wake and make a wider search. He'd get by . . . He'd live through it . . . It wasn't the first time he'd endured a parched throat. Important thing was to catch up with Morg Benson and Lin, meanwhile keeping a sharp lookout for more Apaches.

Moments later he drew up short, halted by the unmistakable sound of a horse stamping as it sought patiently to dislodge the clusters of flies and gnats that plagued him. Gault's first throughts were of Indians. He dropped belly flat in the brush, waited. The sound came again . . . There was a camp ahead, or a party waiting in the undergrowth, as had been the others.

He lay there for a long five minutes, and when he heard no more or saw no movement, he took the hatchet in hand and began to worm his way forward. A dozen yards covered, he halted again. A small clearing lay before him. There were four horses—one was his. He recognized the buckskin instantly.

And then he saw Lin Cooper. Hands bound together, she sat on a fallen log at the edge of the open ground. A rope encircled her waist, was fastened to a nearby tree . . . Morg Benson was apparently taking no chances on her running away.

At the flat, distant report of a gunshot bouncing back and forth between the hills, Jude Worley lifted his thick hand, signaled for a halt. The two men with him drew in close to the gray he rode, their features pulled into frowns.

"Now, who you reckon that is?" Pearce wondered.

"Sounded like one of them old army rifles. You figure there's army around here, Jude?" Damon asked.

"Likely," Worley replied.

His party had dwindled by two. Miles back he'd been forced to let the suffering Pete Bryte head on for Lordsburg where he could get his broken jaw tended to. Link Hazelwood had gone with him—a man alone stood little chance of getting through the Apaches. They'd taken the main road which would put them in the settlement much sooner.

"Could be 'Paches," Pearce said. "Hear they got themselves a right smart of them rifles. Took them off'n dead soldiers."

"Likely," Worley said, again in his laconic, disinterested way.

"Then what the hell we going to do? Sure can't go busting in on no bunch of redskins—just the three of us!"

"Well," Worley drawled, shifting to one side of his saddle in an effort to ease his tortured muscles, "we sure'n hell ain't turning back—not after coming this far."

Rufe Damon stared into the hazy distance. "Maybe it was them running into Apaches. About where they'd be, I figure."

"Yeh, be just our goddammed luck," Pearce grumbled. "Dog them all the way from Colorado, then have a bunch of redskins grab them up!"

"Not them," Worley said dully. "Would've been more shooting . . . Only one shot."

Damon wagged his head. He was badly in need of a haircut, and the curl clusters on his neck were beginning to bother him.

"Don't know about that," he said. "Apaches are mighty tricky critters. Could've jumped them sudden like. Only time for one shot."

"Maybe, but I misdoubt it," Worley said. He sighed heavily. "Come on, let's go. We ain't going to catch up setting here on our butts."

Pearce groaned, spat into the dust. Rufe Damon shrugged.

"Reckon a man can only die once," he said.

## 15

Where was Morg Benson?

Gault lay in the brush, carefully probed the camp with searching eyes. It was a clearing on the edge of a small plateau. Pines and scrubby growth fringed it on three sides; on the fourth the flat appeared to fall away, slide down into a canyon.

Gear had not been removed from the horses, which indicated Benson did not plan to tarry for long—or else they had just arrived. Being short of midday it was unlikely he'd be calling a halt for the night unless, of course, other plans filled his dark mind.

His own buckskin was nearest, Frank saw. Close by stood the black Benson was riding. Lin's bay and Nate Cooper's horse, being used as a pack animal, were on the opposite side of the clearing.

Evidently Benson had the rifle with him. Gault muttered at that bit of ill luck. He'd hoped to lay his hands on the weapon first off. Being without it was like having one arm missing, and he'd need it in the worst way when—and if—they started back for Lordsburg.

He was convinced that Apaches were about in plentiful numbers.

But it wasn't entirely a lost cause. His revolver was in the saddlebags on the buckskin—or had been. It was entirely possible Benson had gone through his gear, discovered the weapon. Gault stirred . . . If so, he'd have to rely on the Apache ax he carried—or, more practical, avoid any conflict at all.

He'd best do that here, he realized. It would be foolhardy to rush into Benson's camp pinning his chances on the pistol that could or could not be there. Smart thing to do was slip in, get Lin, leave fast, taking the two nearest horses. Once away from the clearing, check for the revolver.

Whatever, he'd better act soon. Benson would not be absent for long. Crouched low, Gault fell back, circled to the south end of the camp until he was directly below the girl. Halting, he again surveyed the clearing. Morg Benson was still missing. Lin sat on the log, dejected, forlorn, and tethered like a family pet to the tree.

Taking the knife she'd left for him, he opened the largest blade, and carrying it between his teeth, worked his way hurriedly to where he was immediately behind her. So silent had been his approach that she was totally unaware of his presence until he spoke.

"Don't move."

A faint gasp slipped through her lips as surprise and relief gripped her, but she did not stir.

"I prayed you'd come," she murmured.

Hunched low, he put the knife edge to the leather thongs that locked her hands together.

"You all right?"

The cords parted. She had presence of mind not to move her arms, reveal her freedom.

"I'm all right," she said finally. "Did you—"

"Don't get up until I tell you," he said, slashing at the rope encircling her waist. "Where's Benson?"

"Somewhere down in that canyon. Went to fill the canteens."

He was sweating freely, brushed at his eyes with a forearm. "Been gone long?"

"Yes . . . I think he'll be back any minute now."

"Means we'll have to move fast," he said as the rope dropped away. "I don't have a gun."

She nodded. "He's carrying your rifle. Keeps it with him all the time."

Frank considered the thick brush along the lip of the canyon. "Might be able to hide, jump him when he comes back—"

"No," Lin cut in quickly. "You'd be taking too big a chance—and for nothing. I just want to get away, never see him again."

"Best we start then," Gault said, understanding her fear. "You'll have to ride his horse. Getting to yours would be risky."

"Makes no difference."

"Do just as I tell you. Stand up, step back here into the brush when I give the word. Then turn and run for that big pine you see at the end of the clearing. I'll meet you there with the horses."

She hesitated. "Wouldn't it save time if I went with you—got one of the horses myself?"

"Save time, maybe, but if Benson shows up you'd be in the way. Ready?"

"Ready," she answered, body tensing.

"Now."

Instantly Lin rose, wheeled around the log, and ducked into the undergrowth. Gault had his first glimpse of the discoloration and swelling on the side of her face at that moment, and anger rocked through him.

But there was no time for that. Taking a long stride into the open, he trotted toward the horses. He was suppressing an urge to run, to race into the clearing; he knew his movements must be deliberate, unhurried, otherwise he could frighten the animals, send them shying across the plateau. The buckskin would recognize him, probably wouldn't scare. Benson's horse was a different matter.

He cast a glance to the end of the flat, thinking he heard a sound. There was no indication of Morg. He began to talk to the horses in a low, soothing tone. The buckskin raised his head, looked, resumed his nibbling at the thin grass.

Benson's black seemed not to notice. Gault drew alongside, reached out for the trailing reins, caught them firmly. The black's head came up with a jerk. He tried to pull away, but Frank checked him with a yank on the leathers.

Wheeling, he seized the buckskin's reins, and resisting the impulse to look into his saddlebags for the revolver, moved toward the nearest wall of brush. Both horses, long necks extended, held back, reluctant to be thus led. He broke them loose with a savage jerk.

Gaining the underbrush, dense but not tall enough to screen his movements, he cut right. Again he flung a glance to the rim of the plateau. Benson had not returned.

He skirted the clearing with the horses still objecting, came to the pine where Lin waited. She rushed forward to meet him, and he paused long enough to boost her onto the black, and then pivoted to the buckskin.

The inclination to take time to look for the pistol again entered his mind, and once more he brushed it off. It would require a minute, perhaps two, and if the weapon proved not to be there, that many critical moments would be lost; time enough for Morg Benson to appear, in fact, and stop them. Best to move on, get away from the clearing a safe distance, then look—and hope.

Wheeling the buckskin, he glanced to the girl, pointed. "Hurry! Same trail you came in."

She pounded the black's ribs with her heels, sent him plunging into the brush, but there was a worried frown on her face.

"He'll follow. Can't we go another way?"

"Got to get back on the Lordsburg trail. Only answer is to backtrack."

They could vary it a little, but not enough to be of consequence. The rising bulk of the mountains lay to their left cutting off any possibility of angling through the forest, reaching the trail at some point farther south.

He reached for his canteen and satisfied the thirst that still gnawed at him . . . He wished it were possible to follow a different route. Such would lessen their chances of encountering Apaches as well as the outlaws who surely had drawn closer since dawn. But the long line of towering palisades he'd noted earlier made it clear there was no route open through them. They could do nothing but double back, trust they could avoid all confrontations.

They rode hard, punishing their horses through the scrubby, tangled growth and over the uneven ground. Finally they broke into a lengthy, open meadow where the going was easier. The horses, seemingly anxious to lengthen their stride, now they were unhindered, began to gallop.

Gault turned then to his saddlebags. Unfastening the buckles of the pouch hanging on his right, he jerked back the flap, thrust his hand into its depth. A grin cracked his lips when his fingers touched the cold steel of the weapon.

Pulling it out hastily, he held it canted to one side, spun the cylinder with his thumb. It was fully loaded. Tossing the Apache's ax away, he shoved it under his waistband. Again he probed the leather pouch. There should be a box of cartridges. He found them, and holding the reins between his teeth, unbuttoned the front of his shield-style shirt, tucked the small carton inside.

He felt much better, and swinging in close to Lin, he patted the weapon to show he was no longer unarmed.

"Helps the odds," he said.

She nodded, smiled back. "I'm glad it didn't come to a shooting—with Morg, I mean."

He studied the bruised area on her face. "Owe him for that. How'd it happen?"

"I tried to get away. He caught me. It's nothing." She glanced over her shoulder. "I hope we've seen the last of him."

He signified his agreement. He disliked the man, but there was no real trouble between them—not the sort that warrants a killing, anyway. Morg should now forget Lin, go his way, and give them no problems. The girl had made it plain she wanted nothing to do with him or his plans. If Benson was smart—and man enough—he'd leave it at that. And likely he would unless ... He looked sharply at Lin.

"That money—has Morg got his share?"

The girl glanced to the leather bags hooked over her saddlehorn, turned a despairing face to him.

"I've got it—all of it!"

Frank groaned. They could be sure Benson would follow now. He'd not give up his half of twenty thousand dollars.

"He took it away from me. Said he was going to look after it from here on, hung it on his own horse."

Gault shrugged. If Benson hadn't been so greedy, had left the saddlebags containing the money on Lin's horse where it had been all the time, he'd have it now; nor would they need to worry about him following.

"It's done," he said. "He'll come looking for us. If he catches up we'll try reasoning with him, offer him his share to leave you be—keep going. Maybe he'll use some sense. If not," Gault touched the pistol in his waistband, "maybe I can make him see reason."

Lin shook her head. "I wish he had it all. It's meant nothing but trouble—death, even."

"You're entitled to your share. Your brother worked to get it for you. And you'll need it if you go east."

"If I go," she answered dispiritedly. "It doesn't matter much anymore what I do. I just want to reach a town—see people, feel safe, and try to forget all we've been through."

"Sort of feel that way myself," Gault said, thinking of Tucson and Jud Weatherby. "Ought to be riding into Lordsburg by tomorrow night, or the next morning. That'll end it for you."

His senses pitched to sharp alert. At the far end of the meadow, just within the trees, subtle motion had caught his eye. He stiffened, raised himself partly on the saddle for a better view. He saw it again; the sun glinting against copper bodies fading in and out of the shadows.

"Apaches!" he said in a tight, controlled voice. "Stay close to me!"

# 16

Gault swerved the buckskin hard right. The horse stumbled at the abrupt shift, recovered, thundered on. Frank risked a glance over his shoulder. Lin was right behind him, lips set to a firm line, tanned face pale in the streaming light.

Three braves burst into the open at the end of the field, slanted across the level ground in an obvious effort to cut them off from the protection of the underbrush. Beyond them, and still within the trees, Frank could see others. A fair-sized party . . . a dozen bucks at least . . . maybe more. The thought brushed through his mind that the Apache he'd taken the rifle from had gone all out to recruit help. It was a vagrant thought. This probably was an entirely different bunch.

One of the riders at the end of the meadow extended his rifle, holding it in one hand, stock balanced against his forearm. He pressed off a shot, but the weapon was unsteady and the bullet went far wide.

Frank drew his revolver. They would beat the Apaches to the brush, but what lay beyond was questionable. More Indians, possibly. If so—he looked again to Lin. She was hunched low on the black, was holding him close to the buckskin as he had directed.

The line of brush loomed near. He tried to see into it, separate the shadows, detect any moving shapes. He saw none. Evidently the Apaches had planned a trap at the end of the meadow, intended to let them ride into their midst just as those had done earlier on the trail to him. But one had moved, spoiled the trap . . . Lucky . . . It had saved Lin and him from certain capture, given them an edge.

They reached the brush fringe, plunged into its tangled depths. Instantly Gault swung off, pointing the heaving buckskin for a tall thicket of chokecherry growing in a shallow swale where a creek flowed. It was a long fifty yards distant, and immediately yells broke out and guns began to hammer, filling the basin with echoes.

Frank crouched low on the buckskin, turned to face the three braves quartering in on the left. They presented the most immediate danger. Steadying his hand on his left arm, he leveled the pistol, squeezed off a shot. The nearest Apache wilted, fell heavily from his plunging pony.

The buckskin veered to avoid a rotting stump. Gault, taken unawares, swayed on the saddle, almost lost his balance, caught himself. The two remaining Apaches were still boring in. They were holding their fire, seemingly more interested in simply riding down Lin and Gault.

Frank took close aim, triggered the .44 again. The buck with the blue bandana tied around his head clutched at his middle, sagged, began to swing off. The third, suddenly wanting no more, cut away. Beyond him Frank saw the rest of the party racing in toward the opposite end of the thicket.

What they intended was clear now. The three braves were to drive them into the chokecherries—and into the rest of the party which was sweeping in from the far end of the thicket to meet them head on.

Gault reacted instantly. He cut the buckskin sharp left, bypassing the end of the thicket with no more than a stride to spare. Shots rang out and a burst of yelling warned him that the change of direction had not been missed. But they had the jump on the Apaches now.

Shouting to Lin, he motioned for her to draw abreast so that he would be between her and the Indians, all wheeling about. Grim, he stayed low, hearing the drone of bullets passing nearby, the dull thunk when the lead buried itself in a tree trunk. There were a few repeating rifles in the crowd; the rapid crackle at times was distinctive.

Suddenly two braves, coming in from the opposite side, spurted directly in front of them, paint-streaked faces distorted, mouths open wide as they yelled. Gault fired point-blank at the nearest as the startled buckskin slid to a stop, reared. It was a miss. He pressed off a second shot, saw the brave jolt, fall.

Lin's screams brought him around fast. The second Apache had ridden in close, had a coppery arm around the girl, and was attempting to drag her from her saddle. She was fighting wildly, slamming at the man's face with her small fists. She came off the black. The buck lost his balance at the shift in weight, and both fell to the ground.

Gault was upon them in the next instant, heedless of the screaming, oncoming braves rushing in from the thicket. He smashed his pistol against the Apache's skull, heard the crunch of bone. The man loosened his grip on Lin, fell away.

"Your horse!" Frank yelled at the girl.

She was already turning to the black, reaching for

the saddlehorn. As she swung up, Frank snapped a bullet at the nearest Apache, saw him jar with the impact, fold forward. He fired again—the last cartridge in the .44's cylinder—missed. In that same fragment of time solid force smashed into his arm, half knocked him from the saddle.

He caught a glimpse of the girl's strained, chalky face turned to him, pointed to the depths of the tree-studded basin on ahead.

"Run for it!" he shouted. "I'm—all right!"

Instantly she kicked at the black's flanks, sent him lunging forward. Letting the buckskin's reins hook over the horn, Gault dug into his shirt for the box of extra cartridges. Ignoring the searing pain in his arm, he fumbled for the lid of the small paper carton, managed to hook a thumbnail under its edge, impatiently ripped it open.

Cartridges spilled into the folds of his shirt, and seizing a handful, he struggled to hold the pistol in his numbed left hand while he punched out empties, endeavored to reload with his right.

It was hopeless. Somehow, he was all thumbs. Desperate, he glanced back. The Apaches were almost upon him, their yells dinning in his ears, bullets clipping through the brush around him. It would be only a matter of moments before the buckskin took a slug, went down, or he himself was hit again. He looked to the densely growing trees. Lin was a hunched shape on the black, weaving in and out. She stood a good chance of getting away, and realizing that, he felt better.

Something slapped hard against the side of his head, set him to swaying on the plunging buckskin. His senses wavered, and clutching the pistol tight, he grabbed at the horn of the saddle with his left hand, oblivious of the surging pain the effort caused. He shook his head savagely, tried to clear it of the shadows threatening to close in.

He was vaguely aware of fresh gunfire breaking out on his right. *More of the goddammed bastards,* he thought, and stubbornly fought to stay on the saddle, clear his reeling brain, finish reloading the pistol. If he could get two, maybe three, shells into the cylinder . . . He'd stop a couple more of the screaming devils . . . Letting the buckskin have his head, he struggled with the chore.

The shooting increased. Strangely, he could not hear the lead thudding and clipping around him. The yelling, too, seemed fainter. *Must be losing consciousness. Getting to where I can't hear.* But that didn't jibe with the rest of him somehow. His right hand—fingers worked all right. Shaking his head again, he renewed his efforts to reload, managed finally to insert three cartridges . . . *Now—damn all of you—come on . . . Keep coming.* Hanging on to the horn, he looked back.

The Apaches had swung off, headed for a mound of rocks off a short distance to the north, shooting as they rode. Two men rose from the depths of the mound, dim figures seemingly behind a heavy veil, returned the fire of the onracing Apaches.

The outlaws . . .

The realization reached him through a fog of pain, registered dully on his benumbed brain. He swung back around, searched for Lin. She was ahead, slowing her mount. He waved her on weakly, but she ignored him, pulled the black to a walk. He drew alongside. She stared at his blood-soaked sleeve, the clotted streaks on his face and head. Alarm tightened her features.

"We've got to stop . . . You're hit—need help!"

He shook his head slowly. "No . . . Not out of it yet."

Her lips came together in a tight line, but she kicked at the black, urged him on into the brush. Gault, now steadying himself with both hands on the horn, struggled to maintain consciousness, keep the buckskin close.

"Trail—ought to be—near," he said. "Stay to the left."

Lin nodded her understanding. The shooting behind them had increased its tempo, but it was static, holding to one point. Gault twisted, looked back. No Apaches were following. Their interest had pivoted and now centered on a new enemy. He sagged with relief at that discovery.

Wearily, senses flagging, he resumed his hunched position. Through a haze he saw Lin motion, then cut sharp. They'd reached the main trail. Again he sighed. It would be easier traveling—and faster. And they needed to get out of the basin as quickly as possible . . . No matter which of the warring parties came out the winner of the engagement at the rock-studded mound, their own position would change little. Lin and he were objectives of both.

He guessed they'd have to stop soon. His thoughts were wandering, and the wound in his arm continued to bleed steadily. If he didn't get that stopped, they'd never reach Lordsburg . . . At least, he wouldn't. He stirred impatiently. Be a hell of a thing to bleed to death for something he had no business getting mixed up in.

He became aware that the trail was beginning to slide away, drop into a canyon. Sheer palisades lifted on his left. He stared woodenly at the granite slabs, tried to focus his eyes on the ledges and sharp-edged crevices.

"Got to get up there," he croaked. "Be safe."

Lin peered at him closely. "What?"

"Up there," he said thickly, pointing with his good arm. "Hide—for a while."

"Is there a trail?"

He shook his head. "Don't know . . . Never looked."

Immediately she pulled off the path, and leading the buckskin, began to work her way up the steep slope. She came to a ledge, one high above her head and beyond all possible reach.

"Don't—stop..."

At once she swung left, began to move around the end of the formation. A narrow path appeared, seemed to wind its way through the maze of rocks. A game trail of some sort. Halting, she dropped to the ground. Gault's head lifted questioningly.

"Got to keep... going. A trail... You find one?"

"I found one," Lin replied, and moved on.

## 17

Morg Benson, both canteens filled with fresh water, pulled himself upright and stretched contentedly. Everything was going his way. He had the money—all twenty thousand dollars of it; he'd given the five men on his trail the slip; Frank Gault was dead and out of the running; and he had Lin Cooper.

Somewhere beyond the overlapping ridges and peaks he'd find a town, and where there was a town there'd be a stagecoach line, or at least a road that would take them to where they could board one... And then it was off to New Orleans and a life of luxury and ease.

A warm glow spread through him. Never had he dreamed matters would work out so well! At best he'd planned on half the money and maybe persuading Lin Cooper to become his wife. Had Nate lived that's the way it would have worked out, probably.

But good old Nate was dead and things had changed. All the cash was his, and whether she liked it or not, so was Lin—*if he really wanted her.* That thought occurred suddenly to him, and he fell to giving it serious consideration. He could take her now, or he could leave her—the choice was his. Now that Frank Gault wasn't around, she was forced to depend upon him for everything. That made him feel good, sort of strong and all-powerful.

It was about time, too, that she came to her senses, realized where she stood. She'd changed after they'd met Gault, and he hadn't liked that much. Maybe he'd do a bit of changing himself. Maybe he'd put off this idea of getting married, wait until they reached New Orleans.

Hell, New Orleans was full of pretty women, any of them to be had for the asking if a man had a pocketful of cash to jingle at them. He just might find one there that'd look better to him than Lin Cooper. Yes, sir, that's just what he'd do . . . Wait . . .

Meanwhile, he'd string Lin along, let her think they were getting married. Might as well have all the advantages of being hitched—it was a hell of a long way to New Orleans . . . A lot of nights . . .

And he reckoned he'd as well get that arrangement set up right now. They'd halted in a good spot; make a fine camp even if they weren't near enough to the stream for the horses to water . . . They could last until tomorrow, anyway. Probably be another creek or spring somewhere along the way.

Hooking the canteens over his shoulder, he took up Gault's rifle, propped against a log, and started up the two-hundred-yard-long slope. He was glad he'd come to a decision, elected to spend the night there. Just as well straighten the girl out, have an understanding as to how things were to be between them from there on.

She'd be his wife, only they'd wait until they reached New Orleans to make it all legal and such. He'd explain he wanted to give her a big wedding, a real fancy one. She'd swallow that—and be satisfied.

Halfway up, Morg paused to catch his breath. Something else he'd do before they pulled out in the morning—turn that buckskin of Gault's loose. He didn't want anything around reminding her of him. Seemed like just thinking of him made her sort of bullheaded, hard to handle. Nate's horse could carry the extra gear, and, too, there was a chance they might bump into somebody on the other side of the mountain who'd know Frank Gault, recognize the horse, and make trouble.

He continued on, sweating freely on the grade, came finally to where his eyes were level with the plateau. Abruptly he halted. Something was wrong. Two of the horses were missing—his black and the buckskin. Second thought came to him, and the alarm faded. They'd probably drifted off to graze; he'd find them on the yonder side of the clearing.

He resumed the climb, reached the flat, and moved out of the brush. A fresh surge of anxiety rolled through him. Something *was* wrong! The girl was gone—and she hadn't managed it alone! He could see the rope, ends cut, lying near the log where he'd left her.

Instantly Morg Benson pivoted, ducked back into the brush. Apaches! It had to be. Gault couldn't possibly have gotten loose and come so far so soon—and he was well clear of Worley and his crowd. He was positive he had shaken them.

Crouched in the undergrowth he waited, listened. The Indians could be close by, just holding back until he returned . . . But if it had been Apaches, why hadn't they jumped him when he was down at the creek? And why hadn't they taken all four horses, not just two—Gault's buckskin and his black?

His black!

Goddammit, the money had been on the black! He'd hung the saddlebags on the horse when he took them from the girl. Goddam the lousy luck! If he'd let things alone, let the girl continue to carry the money, he'd still have it.

He knew then it wasn't Apaches. Common sense convinced him of that. They'd have grabbed everything on sight and then come howling down the slope after him, hell-bent on lifting his scalp. And it couldn't have been Frank Gault.

It was Lin herself, all on her own. Somehow she'd managed to use that knife he'd seen her carrying— and forgotten about; she'd cut the thongs he'd wrapped about her wrists, and then the rope he'd tied to the tree. Afterward she'd taken the two handiest horses and headed back. The extra mount was for Gault, of course. She figured he'd still be alive . . . Maybe he was.

A hard grin split his mouth. She must think him a damned fool. He still held all the aces in this little game. He had Gault's rifle, his own pistol—and he'd caught on fast to what she'd done. Hell, she couldn't be more than a mile or so away.

He moved off into the brush at once, still cautious despite his conviction that Lin had engineered her own escape, circled the plateau until he reached the remaining horses. He stood for a brief time debating the wisdom of taking Nate Cooper's black, decided eventually that such would be best, although it would slow him down a bit.

Lin would also be hindered by an extra horse; besides, all their food and gear was on the black, and it would take time to unload, sort and transfer what he had to have to the bay. Thing to do was get on her trail, catch up. He could do whatever changing around he felt was necessary then.

Swinging to the saddle of the bay, he caught up Nate's horse, doubled back across the plateau. Lin wouldn't be traveling fast; she'd have to pick her way since there was no definite trail. It was even possible she'd get herself lost. He swore then, trying to find comfort on a saddle adjusted to fit her smaller body. By God, he'd teach her a lesson she'd never forget when he caught her! She'd not try running off again!

The spiteful crack of a rifle brought Morg Benson to a dead halt. Another gun opened up shortly, and then the wooded basin across which he was riding came alive with echoing yells and gunshots.

What the hell had busted loose? All that shooting couldn't involve Lin. She didn't even have a gun—and if she'd blundered into Apaches, they'd not waste powder and lead on her. They'd simply ride her down, grab her.

The gunshots dwindled, erupted again, farther to the north it seemed. Morg frowned, touched his horse with spurs. It was none of his affair, and if he kept bearing left he'd pass below it. He listened idly to the faint yelling, the quick crackling of the guns.

Apaches, all right, but who—Worley, of course! Jude Worley and his bunch. They'd somehow discovered he'd swung off the main trail, headed east, and were following. Instead of finding him they'd banged smack into a big band of Apaches.

Good! Served them right, goddam them. He hoped the redskins skinned every sonofabitching one of them stone bald . . . And while they were doing it, he'd keep right on moseying along. Lin Cooper and his twenty thousand dollars were not far ahead. The fracas had enabled her to slip by unnoticed, just as it had him, but she had another guess coming if she thought she was going to shake old Morg Benson!

Worley saw the girl and one of the men before the others, hastily curved in behind a thick juniper. Damon and Pearce pulled up beside him quickly.

"What's wrong?" Pearce demanded.

"Here they come," Worley said. "Leastwise, I seen the gal and one of them. Other'n'll be close."

In the next breath Apaches were bursting out of the brush from all directions. Worley watched the girl and the rider swing hard for the brush at the side of the long field they were crossing. Three bucks took after them. Other Apaches were racing to cut them off.

"Let's go," Worley said, and pulled out of the undergrowth, pointing directly for the spot where the Indians would make the interception.

Pearce swore loudly. "We ain't taking on the whole —" he began, but Jude was already spurting into the open.

Immediately the two men followed, dragging out their carbines as, bent low, they started across a narrow strip of grama grass. Ahead the Indians had opened up, and the man with the girl had begun a return fire. Suddenly there was change. The Apaches were veering. They were only dark, fleeting shadows moving through a screen of leaves and branches, but there was no mistaking the fact they were altering course.

"Look out—they're coming this way!" Damon yelled.

Worley cut his horse full left, pointed. "Them rocks over there," he said, cool as if he were ordering a beer in a Telluride saloon. "Good place to make a stand."

Pearce and Damon wheeled in behind him, and in a tight knot they rushed through the pines, reached the ragged upthrust of boulders on a low knoll. They hit the ground as one, raced forward, crowded in close to the granite bulwarks. The Indians had seen them, were already moving in.

Worley steadied his rifle, pressed off a shot. An Apache at the end of the first line of riders dropped from his galloping horse, bounced, arms and legs loose as a rag doll's. Pearce killed the one next to him, but Damon, cursing vividly, was having trouble with the levering mechanism of his weapon.

"Single out the ones with the repeaters," Worley said. "Ain't but three, maybe four, of them."

"Them single shots'll kill you just as dead," Pearce muttered.

"Sure," Worley agreed mildly, "but the jasper looking down the barrel ain't got sixteen chances to do it—only one."

Rufe Damon finally got the action of his carbine freed-up, flattened himself against the rocks, and peered over an edge.

"God in heaven!" he moaned.

There seemed to be Apaches everywhere, whipping back and forth, circling, moving in and out. He could see nothing of the man and the girl, wondered what had happened to them. Probably lying out there dead —just as they'd be soon. He swiped impatiently at the sweat misting his eyes. For chrissake, did Worley expect them to stand off half the Apaches in New Mexico —just the three of them? Hell, there was enough crazy, yelling redskins out there to stomp them to death without doing any shooting!

He brushed at the sweat on his face again, triggered a shot at a brave to his right, saw him waver, levered, nailed another Apache slightly behind the first. He grinned. Worley was right as usual. They had a good place. Maybe they could hold them after all.

"Rufe—behind you!"

At Pearce's warning Damon wheeled, saw the lean, bronze shape of a brave, lance poised, coming in fast. He fired as the Indian launched his spear. The Apache's face disappeared in a mass of exploding blood. It was the last thing Rufe Damon saw in that final instant of time before the lance drove through his chest, pinned him against the rocks.

Pearce glanced at Damon's crumpled body, yelled: "The bastards've got Rufe!"

He watched Jude Worley bob his head, spit. Hunched tight against a flat boulder that stood upright, Jude was in perfect position to cover the little flat in front of the mound. Cool, dispassionate, he was firing mechanically, unmindful of the ear-splitting yells, the confusion of milling horses, the boiling smoke and angry ping of bullets striking stone. Abruptly he paused, turned his head.

"Be smart was you to face the other way, not let them come in from back of us . . . Got plenty of shells?"

Anson Pearce stared at Worley. Jude's impassiveness was just short of inhuman, put chills in your backbone. It was like being partners with a man already dead but who just kept doing things anyway.

"You run short, grab up Rufe's gun," Worley said when Pearce made no reply. "He won't be using it."

Pearce shifted, facing more to the rear as Worley had suggested. The Apaches had pulled back, were gathering in the brush a long hundred yards distant . . . Getting set for a rush . . . Scattered about in between were a half dozen or more who wouldn't be making the try.

Pearce leaned over, picked up Rufe Damon's carbine, laid it across his knees. He'd keep it handy, just in case.

"Here they come," Worley said laconically.

## 18

There no longer was a trail. The faint path had ended, but Lin made no mention of it to Frank Gault. Likely he would not have understood anyway. The wound in his head had dazed him, and he seemed barely conscious. Her greatest fear was that he'd fall from the saddle, further injure himself. And, too, she knew she would be unable to get him back on his horse, once off.

Moving slowly, the sporadic sound of gunfire still echoing across the slopes, she led the horses over the broken rocks and through the tough, wiry brush in a tedious ascent of the steep grade. Now and then she saw tracks in the soft earth; made by deer, she guessed, as they were small, cloven prints, neat and sharp. She was grateful for one thing: they were making little noise. It had rained only recently. Their passage was quiet and they were raising no dust.

She paused. Sheer walls of rock loomed a short distance before her. More lifted on her right. Evidently they'd climbed as high as was possible. She looked around for a place to halt. A slightly lower area to her left offered possibilities.

Forsaking her small cavalcade, Lin made her way through a rocky opening, over a steep if shallow drop, found herself against a hedge of scrub cedar and other short growth. Pushing through, she found herself in a small clearing. It was what she sought.

Returning hurriedly, she led her horse off the ledge, hazing him impatiently through the brush into the open ground. Gault's buckskin, accustomed to a firmer hand, showed reluctance, brought a flush of anger to her cheeks. Picking up a stick of wood, she drove the horse over the embankment into the clearing.

Moving quickly, she assisted Frank to dismount and stretch out on the soft earth along the wall of brush where there was shade from the sun. The horses made it too crowded, and after a bit of exploration, she moved them farther on to a second clearing.

When she returned Gault seemed a little better. He was sitting up, pulling at his shirt, attempting to remove it.

"Hit in the arm. Not bad. Keeps bleeding," he said, looking at her from lackluster eyes.

He seemed unaware of the blood-matted wound on the side of his head.

She said nothing, simply helped him pull off his shirt, the need to backtrack the trail, cover all indications of their movements, pushing at her urgently. The garment removed, she examined the injury. It was not too serious, needed only cleaning and a compress bandage to halt the continuous seeping of blood.

The wound on his head was no worse. A bullet had grazed him, struck a stunning blow, bringing forth a considerable amount of blood, also. It needed no more than cleaning and a bandage. The numbness of his brain would wear off gradually. Both wounds should be treated with a disinfectant, but since they had none, that part of the treatment would have to wait.

First, however, she must look to their safety. As he had looked after her, so now must she protect and care for him while he was helpless. She leaned forward, eyed him closely. The wound in his head no longer bled but there was a steady flow from the ragged hole in his arm.

"I want you to press here," she said, taking his right hand and placing the fingers upon the vein just below the torn flesh. "It'll stop the bleeding."

He stared at her, frowning, started to rise. "Rags in my saddlebags . . . I'll get—fix bandage . . ."

"No, I'll do it," she answered firmly. "Only first I've got to hide our tracks. Someone might try to follow us. Lie there until I get back—it'll only take a few minutes."

She moved off, pushed her way through the underbrush to the trail. Retracing their passage to where a stratum of rock crossed at a right angle, she took up a handful of dry branches and painstakingly wiped out the prints left by the horses.

She continued this precaution all the way to where they had turned off, and there, in an effort to further obliterate signs of their presence, threw dead leaves, small rocks, and bits of litter across the opening until finally no exit at all appeared. Satisfied that she had done everything Frank Gault would have, she returned to the clearing.

He was stronger, more alert, as if the simple application of pressure preventing further loss of blood had benefited him greatly. He greeted her with a sober, almost sullen look.

"Should have left that to me. Don't need a woman doing my chores."

She smiled. His pride was showing and it amused her. "I'll fix up your wounds now . . . You won't mind if I do that?"

He shrugged, gazed off toward the trail. "No sign of the Apaches—or the others?"

Lin shook her head. "The shooting stopped a while back," she said, and hurried to where the horses were grazing.

A sudden concern caught at her. Morg Benson had taken his canteen, and hers, to refill back at the plateau. They would have no water unless . . . Breathing a small prayer she crossed to the buckskin, reached for the container hanging from Gault's saddle. It was heavy, almost full.

Sighing thankfully, she hung it on her shoulder, started to open his saddlebags. Having second thoughts, she removed the leather pouches completely, carried them back to where he lay.

The cleansing should be done with boiling water, but she feared to build a fire. Even if dry, smokeless wood were found, the odor of it would drift down the slopes, be noted by the Apaches, if not by the outlaws or Morg Benson . . . One cheering thing . . . She discovered a pint bottle of whiskey, half full, when digging out the rags. She went ahead then, cleaning the wounds as best she could and disinfecting them with the fiery liquor.

Gault flinched as the application seared his raw flesh, salved the pain with a long pull from the remainder in the bottle while she arranged the bandages. When it was done he settled back with the chagrined look on his face of a self-sufficient man being forced to accept help from someone else.

"Obliged to you."

She was gathering up the items that had been removed from his saddlebags. "That's not necessary—after what you've done for me. Hungry?"

He said, "Some," and glanced to the sun. "Expect we'd best hold off until dark before making a fire."

She frowned. "Aren't you afraid they might smell the smoke even then?"

"There'll be a breeze. Comes in from the west at night. Smoke will go up the rocks."

Lin nodded, paused as another thought came to her. "Food—we don't have any. It was all on Nate's horse."

He pointed to the pouch she had not opened. "Always carry a little. Sometimes get caught out, not close to a town or someplace where I can get a meal."

She opened the pack at once. There was a small quantity of dried beef wrapped in oiled paper, a sack of ground coffee tucked inside a lard tin with which to brew it, two cans of peaches, a bag containing several slices of bread, rock hard.

Lin smiled, considering what he termed a supply of food. It was a wonder he survived if he was forced to rely upon such meager, inadequate supplies very often.

"I'll do what I can when it's dark," she said.

He regarded her with patience. The drink of liquor and the treatment of his wounds had brought swift change to his condition.

"We'll get by," he said.

She rose, went to the horses, and obtained the blanket roll from his saddle. She was almost sorry he was recovering so fast. It would have been pleasant looking after him, having him depend upon her for even a little while. But he was one of those men who resented personal incapability, and that plus the sheer animal vitality of him was going to deny her all possibility of making him her ward for any noticeable time.

By sundown he was up and moving about, flexing his arm gently at first, carefully. The wound in his head seemed not to bother him at all. The firmness had returned to his face and his eyes were again clear and sharp. He walked with her to the edge of the trail, noted her efforts to destroy evidence of their passage.

"Good job," he commented. "Would fool most."

Lin, vaguely injured, looked at him. "Most?"

Gault stirred. "Nobody fools the Apaches when it comes to tracking. They know all the tricks."

He built a fire when it was full dark, scooping out a small hollow behind a tall monolith that would screen the glare from below and waiting until the first light wind began to sweep in from the desert to the west.

They had heard no more gunshots, and Lin knew that such disturbed him, probably because it meant the fighting was over and either the Apaches or the outlaws were on the loose, searching for them . . . Morg Benson was out there somewhere, too.

She prepared the meal, soaking the dried meat and hard bread in water briefly, and then toasting both over the low flames. Gault made the coffee, strong and bitter as gall. They topped off the repast with a can of the peaches, and when they were done she was forced to admit to herself that it hadn't been too bad.

"Are we moving on tonight?" she asked, draining the last in her cup.

"Expect we'd better lay low, give things a chance to simmer down," he said. "Morning early will be soon enough."

She thought of the violent moments back in the basin. "Do you think they're dead—the outlaws, I mean?"

"Hard to say. Odds were with them."

"How can that be? There were so many Apaches. Seemed to be everywhere, yelling, their faces painted—"

"Big party," he admitted, "but they didn't have many good rifles. That's what makes up the difference.

Most of them had old army weapons—single-shot, or else a lance. The outlaws had repeating carbines."

Lin was silent for a time. Then, "I wonder if Morg got caught in the middle of it all?"

"Doubt it. Shooting started before he came along—if he was following us, and I figure he was. Would have been easy for him to swing wide, pass it by."

He got to his feet. Crossing to the opposite side of the clearing, he picked up his blanket, tossed it to her.

"Get some sleep. I'm turning in, too, soon as I've had a look up the trail."

Lin drew the woolen cover about her shoulders, watched him slip into the brush, a lean, silhouetted shape making little noise . . . She'd not had Frank Gault as her own for long—but at least she'd had him for a little while.

# 19

It was still two hours short of daylight when Gault shook Lin Cooper into wakefulness. She sat up, stared around. It was cold, and the pale glow from the sky lent a weird, unreal look to the mountainscape.

"Time to go?" she murmured sleepily.

He had already turned away. "Can't stay here."

She scrambled to her feet as alarm gripped her. "Is there someone coming?" she asked, hurriedly rolling her blanket into a cylinder.

"Horses moving back up in the canyon. Heard them twice."

"Who—"

"Hard to say. Likely Apaches. Best we get out of here before daylight."

Lin said nothing, followed him to the clearing where their mounts waited. He had loosened the saddles, moved them to where the grass was more plentiful. The soaked condition of his hat indicated he had also treated them to a little water.

While he tightened their gear, she lashed her blankets to the saddle, stepped back to watch. His arm was stiff, perhaps even painful, but he went about his task as if oblivious to discomfort. He had removed the bandage from his head, and the only evidence of that injury was a dark streak where blood had dried.

Once or twice during the preparations he paused, listened into the silver-shot darkness, his face turned toward the canyon. At such moments there was a hardness to him, almost a savageness, as if the possibility of further violence, while repugnant and unsought, was welcome to make known its presence if daring to face the consequence.

And then the hard edges of his features would soften, become almost gentle. The brief revelation of scarcely controlled ruthlessness vanished, and he once again was a quiet, cool man going about his work.

"Have to walk the horses down to the trail," he said, handing the reins of the black to Lin. "Can't afford any noise."

He was thinking of the danger to the animals, also. The difficult path up the palisade in full light was risky enough, but in shadow it would be easy for one of their mounts to stumble, break a leg. With no encumbering rider they could make the passage more safely.

They moved out of the clearing, Gault going ahead, leading the buckskin with a short rein. Once beyond the abrupt lip, he halted, waited until the girl had also made the embankment, and then resumed the descent.

Their course was quiet, only an occasional click of steel against stone when one of the horses put a hoof against rock, but that, too, was muted in the eerie stillness of the mountain. They reached the foot of the slope. Gault stopped, ground-reined the buckskin, and turned to Lin.

"Wait," he said.

He trotted up-trail a short distance, paused and stood for a time listening while his eyes restlessly searched the canyons and the hillsides. He returned shortly, made a similar survey of the country below them.

"Nobody around, seems," he said, coming back to where she waited. "But we'll not gamble on it."

He caught her by the elbow, helped her to the saddle, and swung onto the buckskin.

"Stick close to the inside of the trail. Less likely to be seen."

She nodded soberly, asked the same question she'd put to him earlier. "Who do you think's out there?"

"Apaches—the outlaws—Morg Benson, maybe. Could be any of them—or all. No way of knowing."

They moved off. Lin glanced over her shoulder, trembled violently. "Nothing's really changed then, has it? They could all be hunting us, waiting somewhere—maybe around the next bend—"

"About the size of it."

A small sound of hopelessness broke from her lips. "Oh, I wish it would end! I wish it had never started . . . All this running and hiding—the killing . . ."

"Be over—pretty soon."

Lin's head came up. "Lordsburg? How far?"

"Ought to reach there tomorrow."

He started to say more, explain that the estimate hinged solely upon the luck, good or bad, they encountered in the miles that yet remained, but dropped it.

"Tomorrow," Lin repeated in a falling voice. "A long time."

"We'll make it," Gault said confidently.

He was a high, squared shape before her in the half-dark, apparently realized suddenly that he was carrying himself rigidly, favoring his arm.

"Your wound! It's bothering you."

He merely shrugged. "Nothing to worry about. I'll get over it."

They pressed on, following the narrow trail now climbing a long slope, next dipping into a deep swale where brush crowded in on both sides; again crossing a high grass-covered saddle that swung gracefully from one towering peak to another.

A coyote loped in front of them for a brief spell, bushy tail dropped, head shifting back and forth as he skulked the shadows in search of food. Once an owl, startled from a perch by their passing, swooped low, almost brushing Lin's face with its wing tips. She gave a little frightened yelp, and then laughed to ease the tension.

It was growing lighter. Beyond the ridges to the east a pale gray was making an appearance, spreading upward in an ever-enlarging fan, creeping silently toward the center of the heavens. The dark pockets in the brush were beginning to fade, and other things, mysterious in the night, were taking shape, becoming familiar.

Gault looked back to Lin. "Stop for coffee first chance we get. Eat a bite, too, if you're hungry."

She smiled. "No need."

"Ought to have coffee," he replied.

A moment later he pulled to a halt, raised himself on the saddle. The girl moved up beside him, features reflecting her quick worry.

"What—"

He silenced her with a lifted hand. For a time there was only the faintly rustling brush stirred by the breeze, the muttering of birds rousing for the day, and then he heard again the warning sound: the quiet thud of horses' hooves upon the packed earth.

Instantly he dropped back into place. Beckoning to the girl, he wheeled off the road, spurred the buckskin into the undergrowth. A dozen paces and he veered south, heading into the direction of the sound but getting a distance below the point where they had quit the trail. Well hidden in the junipers and other growth, Gault hunched forward on his horse, waited, eyes on the trail ten yards below them.

The minutes dragged. Lin's black shifted restlessly. Gault reached out, laid a hand on the horse's neck, began to rub slowly as he sought to quiet the animal.

Abruptly there was motion at the end of the narrow, aisle-like view they had of the trail. An Apache, legs dangling loosely at the flanks of his pony, head dropped forward, crossed the opening, vanished. Another appeared. A third—and more until Frank had counted seven.

He turned, grinned bleakly at the girl. "Close," he murmured. "Too close."

She was staring after the departed Indians. "Won't they notice our tracks?"

"Little dark yet, and they're not looking for any. Lucky the wind was against us. Never heard us coming."

"Must be going to join the others—what's left of them."

"Maybe. Most likely a different bunch. Country's overrun with them." He hesitated, added as an afterthought: "Glad they didn't come along yesterday."

He started the buckskin back through the brush, approaching the trail at a slant. A few paces short he again halted, and once more raising himself in his stirrups, had his long look at the slope across which the path wound its way.

"They're gone," he said, relaxing, and then smiling, pointed ahead. "We get to the yonder side of that hill we'll stop, make that coffee."

Jude Worley and Anson Pearce saw the seven Apaches, too.

Around three that morning, well before first light,

they had moved from their place in the rocks where they had made a stand, and ridden out of the basin, striking south along the trail to Lordsburg.

"We seen two of them heading this way, didn't we?" Worley replied when Pearce had remarked on it. "And they sure'n hell wouldn't go north."

As to the third member, neither was certain whether he had joined the pair later or not. It was a likely possibility. Everything was in such a state of wild confusion after they bumped into the Apaches that the other man could have been somewhere around all the time and they'd simply missed seeing him.

It had been a lousy streak of luck that brought the Indians into the scene just as they were closing in on the trio. Worse luck yet that Rufe Damon had been killed during the fight that followed.

But there were a few Apaches who wouldn't be riding the hills, killing and raising hell in the days to come. Jude took strong satisfaction in that knowledge. It had been a devil of a scrap with the difference coming only from the sort of weapons he and Pearce were using. Story would have ended another way if the Apaches had all been using modern carbines, or he and Pearce had been caught with just their sixguns.

That last rush had almost finished them off despite their superior equipment. The Indians, still a dozen or so strong, had come in at them from three sides. That's when Pearce took an arrow in the leg. Worley, too, had mementos of that rush. A bullet had splintered rock close to his face, peppered him with sharp fragments and started him to bleeding in a dozen different places like a stuck hog.

But they'd turned the bastards back, knocking at least half of them off their ponies, knowing they had to do it, or die. The rest of the braves had swung off into the brush and just sat there, unwilling to make another try and not wanting to give it up, either.

Just to let the two men in the rocks know they were still around, every now and then one of them would pick up his rifle and throw a bullet into the mound. No damage was ever caused by such, but it did play hell with a man's nerves.

Worley finally decided the braves had just holed up, were waiting for daylight or for more of their kin to come along, and figured they'd best move on. They buried Damon there, hollowing out a grave below a tall slab of granite and then covering him over with loose rock so the wild animals couldn't get to him.

Shortly after that they pulled out, leading their horses through the brush, keeping always in the dark out of the moonlight. The Apaches made no effort to follow, and Worley guessed either their movements went unnoticed or else the Indians had left ahead of them. It didn't matter. He was just damned glad to get out of there.

They mounted up when they'd covered a safe distance, but still taking care to make little noise and not expose themselves unduly, rode across the basin to where they joined the trail. They reached there just as the sky was beginning to pearl.

They struck southward at a steady trot. The girl and her companions were ahead of them—how far only God knew. But that was a matter of no consequence to Jude Worley. He'd catch up—eventually.

Not much later they spotted the seven Apaches coming up the trail a half mile distant. At once he and Pearce peeled off into the dense undergrowth and lay there until the braves had passed.

When a proper time had elapsed, they returned to the path and doggedly resumed the chase; Worley, face splotched with blood where the granite splinters had pierced his skin, jaw set, eyes sullen and grim; Pearce, suffering in silence with the head of an arrow buried deep in the calf of his leg.

He'd hoped earlier to stop, burn a knife point, and

dig the goddammed thing out, but Jude had shaken his head, refused.

"We ain't got no time to waste," he'd said.

## 20

Miles to the south Morg Benson, sprawled at the base of a sandstone talus, and well hidden by the accumulation of fragments, also watched the seven Apaches file by.

He had crouched in his fortress of rock, rested Gault's rifle upon a convenient boulder, and sighting down the barrel, thought how easily he could pick them off, one by one. Be no trick to get them all—probably before any of them could figure where the shots were coming from.

But Morg wasn't interested in killing Apaches and thereby betraying his hiding place. He was waiting for Lin Cooper and Gault. They'd be coming along soon, and he'd be ready for them.

He'd started out after them when that other bunch of Indians had run into Jude Worley and his crowd. That had been a lucky break for him; he'd been able to slip by unnoticed by either party and thus get right on the trail of Gault and the girl. They'd played it smart, too, taking advantage of all the shooting and confusion to get out of that basin.

But he'd overshot them on the trail. Evidently they'd turned off, holed up for the night. That was a bit strange. He figured once they were clear of the Apaches they'd line out fast for Lordsburg, and while he wasn't much at reading tracks, he did see where two horses had swung onto the trail and headed south.

Then he lost the sign. For some reason they'd halted . . . Maybe the Apaches had managed to get a bullet into one of them, forcing them to stop . . . It didn't matter. As soon as he realized and knew for certain he was between them and Lordsburg, he'd looked around, found a spot where he had a good view of the country, and pulled up. All he need do now was sit tight until they came along.

He grinned, thinking of the jackpot Gault and the girl had jockeyed themselves into. That goddammed Gault thought he was so smart! He didn't know it but he was caught smack in the middle—the Apaches or Jude Worley, maybe both, in back of him; old Morg Benson in front . . . One thing for sure, Mr. Frank Gault would never see Lordsburg, only he didn't know it yet.

He caught sight of them not long after the string of Apaches had trickled by, two small specks, indistinct in the dull light, but there was no doubt in his mind as to their identity. He could spot Lin Cooper a mile off—hell, he'd had his eye on her for years, hadn't he? A slow grin spread across his florid face.

Gault was on his buckskin and in the lead. The girl was not far behind. Gault was being careful, keeping a sharp watch on the country around them. Probably afraid there'd be more Apaches come along . . . Man couldn't blame him for wanting to reach Lordsburg. Having twenty thousand dollars and a gal such as Lin Cooper drop into your lap was like having a banker open up his safe and telling you to help yourself.

He guessed he'd fooled them completely, getting out in front of them the way he had. They probably figured he was laying dead back there in the basin; or maybe they thought he'd just saddle up and keep going back there at the plateau when he found both the girl and the money gone.

He had news for them. They didn't know Morg

Benson. Nothing was knocking him out of that money—and the bonus that went with it, Lin Cooper. Both belonged to him and he meant to collect . . . And right now he was sitting mighty pretty to do just that.

He had Gault's rifle, leaving the man unarmed and helpless as a lamb. Grabbing that gun had about the same effect on Gault as cutting off both hands at the wrists . . . It was going to be a cinch.

He watched Gault and Lin Cooper dip down into a steep arroyo and disappear behind an intervening hill. Immediately he rose, and swinging to the saddle, rode the short distance to the edge of the trail where the brush was thick, and dismounted.

Hiding his horse well back where it could not possibly draw attention, and rifle in hand, he worked his way to the bulge of rock he'd selected earlier as the place where he would wait once he saw them coming. He licked his lips, picturing in his mind the surprise both would evince when he calmly stepped from behind the granite shoulder. The looks on their faces would be something he'd remember and enjoy for years.

Savoring the expected moments, he levered the rifle, made certain a cartridge was in the chamber, and eased back. Dawn had finally broken, sending long fingers of color reaching into the sky and bringing a promise of heat. He was getting close to the desert, he realized. Be good to reach Lordsburg, cool off in a saloon with a few beers.

He heard them before he saw them—the faint, regular thud of hooves, and then moments later the dry creak of saddle leather. Stiff, tense, he allowed them to pass the pile of boulders, being certain not to make his move too soon. When they were by, he cocked the carbine and stepped out onto the trail.

"Far as you go, Gault!"

Surprise and fright exploded a small cry from Lin Cooper's lips. Frank Gault simply halted, froze.

"Morg!" the girl exclaimed, wheeling her horse around.

"Yes, ma'am—Morg!" Benson parroted smugly, enjoying each pulsating instant. "Reckon you didn't expect me. Figured you'd give me the slip—and with all that money. Bet you was even hoping I was dead back there with all them others."

Benson paused, shifted his gaze to Gault's broad back. "Why ain't you saying something, mister? Ain't you a mite surprised, too?"

"Got over ever being surprised years ago," Frank answered.

Morg's face flushed deeper and his eyes flared. "Still the big, tough cowboy, eh?" he snapped, his manner changing. "Well, you're going to learn something here today, friend . . . Be a lesson you'll remember to your dying day. Step down off that horse."

Frank Gault leaned forward slightly, made some adjustment with the front of his brush jacket, and came off the saddle slowly. Wheeling, he faced Morg.

Benson nodded, said: "Just stand easy . . . And you," he added, shifting his glance to the girl, "set right where you are. We'll be moving on right quick —soon as I take care of this little job."

Lin's eyes, filled with fear, swung to Frank Gault. He was watching Benson with steady intent, arms folded across his chest.

"If you're thinking about pulling the trigger of that rifle, don't do it," he said quietly. "One shot and you'll have every Apache within hearing distance down on your neck before you can go a mile."

Benson's head thrust forward. "You mean that bunch that rode by here? Seen them. Don't reckon they'll give me no trouble. They're a far piece up the road by now."

"Not far enough . . . And there are plenty others. Think of Lin . . . You want her falling into their hands?"

"She won't. I'll be seeing to that."

"Morg," the girl said suddenly, moving closer and laying her hand on the leather bags slung across her saddle. "The money's right here. It's yours—all of it. Just let us go."

Benson's lips curled. "Heard you singing that song before—and the answer's still no. What're you so allfired worked up about, anyway? Ain't nothing bad going to happen to you. Just ain't in my figuring. Sure, I'm a mite peeved at you, running out the way you did—"

"Please, Morg—"

Benson's thick brows arched. "It him you're begging for? That it? You don't want me putting a bullet through his head, giving him what's coming to him for butting in—that it?"

Lin nodded brokenly. "He doesn't deserve anything like that . . . He was only helping me—you, too, really. You know that."

"Helped at first 'til he heard about the money and set his eyes on you. Then he wasn't helping nobody but himself."

"That's not true. He didn't want to get mixed up in it at all. We—I forced him to—forced him to stay with us all along when he could have gone on after Nate died . . . You can't—"

"I can do any goddammed thing I want," Benson cut in, waggling the rifle. "And one of them is squaring up with him. Don't like getting pushed around, same as I plain don't like him."

"Better forget it," Gault said evenly. "You've got other problems right now."

Morg laughed. "You trying to pull that old trick on me—make me think somebody's coming? Them Apaches, maybe?"

Gault said nothing, continued to stare at the trail beyond Benson. In the next moment Lin Cooper stiffened with fear.

"The outlaws—they've caught up!"

Benson looked at her in disbelief as if thinking

perhaps she was adding credence to Frank Gault's attempt at deception. But he turned his head, anyway. He saw the two men moving down upon him, picking their way on foot through the brush.

"Worley!" he yelled.

Gault acted swiftly. Pivoting, he slapped Lin's black sharply on the rump, sent it plunging off down the trail.

"No, goddam you!" Benson shouted, coming back around. "You ain't getting away with—"

Gault spun again. One hand swept aside the front of his jacket, the other came up fast with the revolver tucked in his waistband. He shot Benson twice in the chest before the man could trigger the rifle, and then leaping aside, vaulted onto the buckskin.

Immediately Worley and the man with him opened up, but Frank Gault had already rounded the shoulder of rock, was racing to overtake Lin Cooper now well down the slope.

# 21

Gault gave no thought to the rifle shots flatting above the drumming hooves of the galloping buckskin. The outlaws were wasting lead. The bulge behind which Morg Benson had hidden was serving a different purpose now—shielding Lin and him, preventing the men from getting an open shot.

He looked beyond the straining buckskin's head. Lin was slowing, allowing him to overtake her. A few moments and he was near, and then together they raced on down the long grade, following the winding path for a considerable distance before it again curved toward the rugged hills.

Both horses were sucking for wind after the fast flight. Gault began to pull up, motioned for Lin to do the same. She complied immediately, but her face wore a worried frown.

"Those outlaws—"

"They'll have to go back for their horses. That'll give us a fair lead."

He hadn't noticed where the men had left their mounts. Apparently it had been some distance back on the trail . . . And there were only two of them now . . . Five in the beginning . . . Evidently they'd had a bad time of it with the Apaches. He felt Lin Cooper's eyes on him, returned her look questioningly.

"Morg—is he—"

Gault nodded. "Gave me no choice."

The girl shuddered, and then she smiled wanly. "I know. I'm not blaming you. It's only that now there's another death because of the money."

"Only a couple of those outlaws left in the running, too, seems."

"It's been a terrible thing—almost like the gold, the money, was cursed . . . I'm beginning to wonder now if we'll live to reach Lordsburg."

Gault said nothing. The settlement was still far in the distance; beyond the hills ahead, beyond White Rock Canyon, beyond the plains that came after. It would take all that day and well into the next—and luck.

"This canyon—the one you told me about," Lin said. "Once we're past it will we be safe?"

He shrugged. "No guarantee anywhere in this country of that now, but our chances ought to be better."

The probability of not encountering Indians beyond White Rock Canyon was better; they preferred to avoid the plains, but he was thinking mostly of the outlaws. They would recognize no stopping point. They had followed this far; they'd not quit now.

He glanced back. Two riders, so distant as to be indistinguishable, were moving up the trail doggedly, relentlessly. Lin saw them, too, and he watched her lips tighten.

"They'll not get any closer than they are," he said, hoping to allay her fears.

The end of a short meadow was before them, and shortly they began a climb into a maze of jagged, peaked upthrusts of glistening granite. "Castlerocks," he recalled someone had named the area, but he remembered it only as a hell of a place to get caught when the sun was high.

The walls of stone caught the burning rays, filled the narrow passageways through which the trail wound with stifling, searing heat. They were fortunate; they were crossing while it was still fairly cool.

The horses were laboring and soaked with sweat when they reached the summit. They couldn't go much farther without rest, outlaws or not. Gault pointed to a cluster of gray-green at the foot of the grade now sliding away before them.

"We'll stop there."

At once Lin showed alarm. "But those men—"

"Their horses are in no better shape than ours. Have to spell them. When we see them come over the top of the hill, we'll move on."

The plan afforded them almost an hour's respite. During that time Lin made coffee and broke out some of the dry food and the last can of peaches in Gault's saddlebags. While she was busy at that, he cared for the horses, loosening the tack, giving them a little water from their diminishing supply by pouring it on a rag and squeezing it into their mouths.

The rest period, however brief, proved effective, and when the two outlaws appeared on the skyline, they mounted and resumed the trail with their horses showing renewed strength.

Soon they topped out another ridge, and looking back, saw the men just entering the field where they had paused. Whether they, too, would halt to breathe their fagged animals was a question—one to which Frank Gault elected not to wait for the answer.

Near the middle of the hot afternoon they reached the mouth of White Rock Canyon, a mile long cleavage in the brown earth, along the eastern side of which an eyebrow trail clung precariously.

They drew up a short distance within the narrow rock-filled gash now steaming with the day's heat, and Lin had her first view of its depths and of the trail, wide enough only for the passing of a single horse. He recognized her thoughts.

"It'll be all right. Gone through here myself a dozen times. Plenty others use it, too."

But he assured her with misgivings. The rains had visited White Rock Canyon, and with considerable violence. He noted the washes were cut deeper; trees that once stood proud were now uprooted, lay on the steep slope of the canyon below—the leaves of most still green, which attested to the recent presence of the storms.

And the trail itself . . . The edge was rounded where soil had sloughed away. Here and there a deep gouge in its surface marked the point where water had cascaded from higher ledges, cut channels with destructive force.

But there was no alternate route, no turning back unless he wanted to risk a showdown with the outlaws —one revolver against two long-range rifles. He glanced at Lin, masked his concern with a grin.

"Sooner we get to the other end, the sooner we'll reach Lordsburg."

"Whenever you're ready," Lin replied.

He led off at once, holding the buckskin close to the rock face of the cliff. Lin moved in behind him, carefully following in the gelding's tracks.

For the first hundred yards Gault moved with caution, watching the soil, listening for crumbling edges and falling rocks that would indicate an unsafe condition. But the footing seemed firm, and after a time he felt a lessening of tension. Mopping sweat from his forehead, he glanced to Lin. She, too, was feeling more confident, the first moments of fear having passed.

"Let your horse have his head," Frank called. "He knows what has to be done."

She smiled and they pressed on, barely crawling, it seemed. The trail narrowed, widened, slimmed again where a great chunk had slipped and plunged to the bottom of the canyon. A grimness came over Gault again, but he kept it from the girl.

High overhead an eagle soared in effortless ease, wings set, circling tirelessly. There was no other sign of life in the breathlessly hot confines of the deep gash, however; it was as if they'd entered an abandoned world.

Halfway...

The overhanging cedar that protruded from the cliff, marking that specific point, had been ripped loose, now lay on the trail at the foot of the steep wall of stone. The horses moved by it gingerly, forced to step over the withering branches. Gault stared ahead thoughtfully. It seemed to him the trail was narrowing and now slanted toward the bottom of the canyon. The storms had struck hardest in this section.

He reached down, patted the tired buckskin. A great deal would depend on the horse and his innate sense of danger from there on. He'd halt, refuse to continue if, warned by that mysterious perceptive ability bestowed upon all animals by nature, he felt the footing unsafe.

The minutes wore on as they moved at a snail's pace across the near vertical slope. The heat was monstrous. Gault was clothed with sweat and the horses appeared dark, wet, hair plastered to their lathered bodies. Lin brushed at her eyes continually, occasionally fanned herself with her hat.

Three quarters of the way behind them. Gault turned, started to reassure Lin with that bit of information. The words died in his throat as a rifle shot reverberated through the canyon.

Surprised, startled, Gault rose in his stirrups, looked back. The outlaws . . . They'd reached the mouth of the canyon, were entering. They had not halted to rest their mounts, as he'd expected, instead had pushed on ignoring their faltering horses, punishing them cruelly in a final, desperate effort to catch up.

The canyon echoed again. The distance was considerable, and any degree of accuracy on the part of the men was impossible. The bullets were striking somewhere behind and overhead, sending down small rivers of gravel and soil spilling onto the trail.

A tenseness gripped Frank Gault. With the steep slope softened by heavy rains, a bullet could cause a landslide. He squinted anxiously ahead. He could see the end of the path, see where it broke out onto a flat where pines grew tall and thick.

He tried to judge the intervening ground, wondering if he dare force the horses into a hard, fast run and gain safe footing quickly. Or would it be better to go slow, be certain? If a slide resulted they could then make a dash for it.

In that next moment the decision was made for him. The outlaws, determined to force them to halt, pin them against the rocks, opened up in unison. Bullets slammed rapidly into the face of the cliff above and around Gault and the girl, several coming dangerously close.

Rocks and dirt began to pour down upon the trail, a little at first and then increasing. A low rumbling filled the air, rising swiftly in strength, soon overriding the echoes of the furious gunshots. Gault threw a hurried glance to the crest above him, turned to Lin.

"Come on!" he yelled, galvanized into sudden action by what he saw.

Jamming spurs into the nervous buckskin, bent low, he began a race for the end of the canyon. He could hear the hammering of Lin's black close behind, heard faintly another volley of gunfire—and then all was swallowed up in a vast, roaring thunder.

A blast of hot wind struck them, and the sound of plunging rocks, sliding earth, the crackling and crashing of trees, was a world within itself. A huge cloud of dust lifted, stirred from depths untouched for centuries by storms, began to spread out over the canyon, fill its depth, build up in layers above it, blocking out the sun.

Through the choking haze Gault saw the tips of the pines stirring violently as the wind rushed through them. He wiped at his eyes, searched for Lin. She was near, her face tipped down, strained. She was leaving it all to the black horse.

"Not far!" Gault yelled above the now dwindling roar.

She nodded but he was unsure whether she understood or had simply acknowledged his attention. And then in the next lunging stride of the buckskin, he felt the solidness of the flat under the gelding's hooves and knew that they had made it.

He pulled up short, spun to meet the girl. She was beside him before he came completely around, choking, gasping, dust clinging to her in a filmy, tan cloak. She brushed at her eyes, produced a wry smile.

"Close—too damned close," she said, quoting words he had earlier used.

He grinned, nodded. "For sure."

Lifting his glance he looked back into the still-swirling, dust-choked depths of the gash. "No need to hurry now. They can't follow."

The trail through White Rock Canyon no longer existed.

## 22

"Lordsburg," Gault said, pointing toward a grayish smudge at the far edge of the long slope down which they rode.

They had spent the night in a coulee not far south of White Rock Canyon, too weary to continue, for, as he had said, there was no reason to hurry. Only Apaches were a threat, and considering the area in which they had halted, that was a minor one.

They had little water, less food, but they made out. The main street of Lordsburg would be under their feet by noon of that next day and that thought alone was sustenance.

"Seems months since I left Colorado," Lin said wistfully as they pushed on steadily. "Months since I had a bath, a decent meal—even saw a town with people. And when I think of what all has happened—" She hesitated, turned impulsively to Gault. "Oh, Frank, I'm so thankful we ran into you! I'm afraid to think what would have—"

"You'd have made out," he said. "Folks always do, somehow."

She stared off over the plains in moody silence then. The sun was high, but a scatter of clouds was making for some coolness.

"What will you do when we get to Lordsburg?"

"Keep going, I expect," he said. He made no mention of the long-hoped-for job with Jud Weatherby and the fact that it likely was lost to him, this time for good. "May try my luck in California. Lot going on out there. What'll you do?"

"I don't know . . . I really don't."

"You're a rich woman," he said, smiling. "Shouldn't have any problem. You can go anywhere, do most anything you like."

"Somehow that doesn't mean much anymore. Maybe if Nate were still alive—and Morg—"

He glanced at her sharply. "Thought Benson meant nothing to you."

Lin gave him a quick, puzzled look, then shook her head. "He didn't. I'm trying to say that if they both were still alive, there'd still be a purpose to coming here—a reason for it."

She turned again to Frank. "Morg Benson was nothing to me; only I never realized that until I saw him for what he was. Up to then I just went along, overlooking everything, taking things for granted, and as they came. I guess when it comes right down to it, I never thought about anything much—just left it all up to Nate."

He was quiet, seemingly engrossed in the consideration of her words. Finally he stirred, brushed back his hat, and mopped at his face with a forearm.

"Lordsburg's not much," he said, the harshness gone from his voice. "Don't expect you'll want to stay around long. If you like, I'll arrange for your stage passage, get you on your way—Maryland, wasn't it, where you're from. Or you aiming to go back to Colorado?"

"No, not Colorado. And there's no reason to go to Maryland. No one's there. I—I don't know what I want to do."

He studied her for a time, his face set to quiet lines, his eyes almost soft. Then: "No big rush to decide. After a couple of nights' rest, that bath you talked about, and some good grub, things'll look different."

Her face was sober when she returned his gaze. "I wonder," she said desolately.

He was having his own thoughts about Lordsburg

and what their arrival would mean to him. It would seem strange not having Lin with him; not having her to think about, plan for, worry over . . . But he reckoned he'd get over it.

All things pass, the good and the bad, and time would doubtless come when she would have slipped entirely from his memory. The remembrance of other women had. There was no reason to think Lin Cooper would be any different.

Or was there? He found himself pondering that, almost fighting to convince himself of its truth. It had to be that way, he told himself. He hoped, however, that there would be a stagecoach departing for somewhere soon after their arrival. The quicker she was aboard and bound for some distant destination, the better for him.

Along toward the middle of the afternoon with the sun now laying bands of shimmering heat over the flat country, they crossed the last of the sandy washes and came to Lordsburg's outskirts—a thin scatter of sagging adobe huts crouched beneath a few water-starved trees.

"Main part of town looks better," Gault said apologetically, and then frowned as three men stepped from a jacal on their right, fanned out to form a barrier across the road. One, a bristle-bearded individual with a thick moustache to match, wore a star pinned to his shirt. The others were vaguely familiar. All had drawn their pistols.

"Raise your hands—both of you!" the lawman ordered with no preliminaries.

Surprise gave way to anger in Frank Gault. Ignoring the command, he cupped his hands on the horn of his saddle and regarded the marshal coldly.

"You've got your ropes crossed, mister. What's this all about?"

"You know without asking," the lawman snapped.

"I'm Kingston, Lordsburg town marshal. Been waiting for you to show up. Where's your partner?"

"Partner?" Frank echoed, and then heard Lin gasp faintly.

"Those two men with him . . . I know them. They're some of the outlaws."

Gault remembered then. He'd seen the pair right at the start. The one with the bandaged jaw—he was the one who'd been holding the horses that first night in the arroyo. Evidently Worley, or whatever the name of the gang's leader was, had sent these two on ahead by the road in event he and the others failed to overtake the Cooper party. They had convinced the local lawman with some sort of cock-and-bull story, swung him to their side.

"Don't know what you've been told, Kingston," he said, "but that pair with you are outlaws. We've been dodging them for days."

"Outlaws!" the marshal exclaimed, his mouth flying open. "By God, you've got the guts of a mule! They're deputies—both of them. Part of Sheriff Worley's posse from up Colorado way!"

## 23

Frank Gault was rigid on his saddle. The lawman's words hammered at him dully.

"Posse?"

"Don't go making out like you didn't know," the deputy at Kingston's left said. "Been chasing you ever since you robbed that bank."

Gault turned slowly, disbelievingly to Lin Cooper. She met his eyes unwaveringly.

"I—I didn't know," she said in a stricken voice. "They told me—Nate and Morg—that—"

She hadn't known. He realized that instantly. Lin had been duped, even as had he. Nate and Benson had robbed a bank somewhere, explained their sudden wealth to her as gold they'd taken from their mine. It explained, too, their need to leave Colorado suddenly. He brought his attention back to Kingston.

"Maybe there was a robbery, Marshal," he said quietly, "but the lady here, and me—we don't know anything about it. The men you're looking for are dead."

"Maybe one is—you're not."

"No, both of them. My name's Gault. Just happened along, got mixed up with them. Lady's in the same fix. You want to find out for sure, send a telegram to the marshal in Dodge City, ask him about me."

Some of the hostility slipped from Kingston's big frame. He turned to the man who had spoken.

"You ever see these people before, Hazelwood?"

The deputy nodded. "Sure. Recognize the woman. She was riding with Benson and the other robber . . . Don't seem like it was this fellow, though."

"But you're sure she's the woman?"

"Reckon I am. You can wait 'til Worley and the others get here, make certain."

Kingston's face hardened again. "What about the sheriff and the others? Where are they?"

Gault ducked his head toward the mountains. "Back there somewhere. Trail through the canyon caved in ahead of them. They'll have to double back, come in by the road. Only two of them. Apaches got one."

"Or maybe it was you," Hazelwood said, "and that's how you got bunged up, shooting it out with them." The deputy paused, glanced to Kingston. "I got a hunch he's mixed up in it plenty, Marshal. Probably was waiting for them, had a fast getaway all fixed. Probably heading into Mexico."

"You're a damned fool," Gault said softly, flatly. "Telegram to Dodge will prove it."

Kingston sighed gustily. "Well, Worley can figure it all out when he gets here. One thing—there ain't no sense standing out here in the sun hashing—"

"The money—where is it?" Hazelwood broke in as if remembering suddenly.

Kingston caught himself. "Yeh, where is it? Twenty thousand dollars, I'm told."

Gault shifted slightly, removed his hands from the saddlehorn. Reaching out with his left, he lifted the saddlebags from Lin's horse.

"Right here," he said, and flung the pouches straight at the lawmen.

Kingston and the two deputies dodged involuntarily. In that moment of confusion Gault's pistol came out fast, laid its threat upon them.

"Don't like doing this, Marshal," he said. "But you're not giving me much choice."

Anger flushed Kingston's broad face. "Should've figured you'd have a hide-out gun . . . Best you drop it. This'll get you nowhere."

"It's getting both of us to Tucson," Frank said. "I've told you the truth. Neither one of us had anything to do with that bank robbery. Just got ourselves suckered in on it by the men who pulled it off. They're both dead—and you've got the stolen money. I figure that ought to satisfy you and this Worley."

"It ain't going—"

"Now, we're riding on to Tucson. Could be I've still got a job waiting for me there. Not sure. Meanwhile you send that telegram to Dodge City. If what you find out doesn't put me in the clear, along with the lady on my say-so, then come to Tucson. Either I'll be there or the marshal will know where to find me."

Kingston stared at Gault for a long minute. His eyes touched the pistol in Frank's hand. He shrugged.

"Not much else I can do."

Again there was a dragging silence. Finally Hazelwood said: "Could be he's telling the truth. He don't look like either one of them we was chasing. And they didn't show up with these two. Could be dead."

"Worley will tell you one is. Was there when I— when he died. Other man's back up the trail a ways. Helped bury him myself. One of your posse members put a bullet in him."

The deputy with the bandaged jaw, speaking with difficulty, nodded at Lin. "Far as she goes, there wasn't no woman along when that bank was robbed. Only two men."

"All right then, Gault," Kingston said with finality. "It'll be your way. You and the woman can move on . . . But if you're lying, look for me to show up in Tucson."

"Won't have trouble finding me. Now, all of you, drop your guns. Start walking for town."

The lawman stiffened in outrage. "The hell I—"

"Let's don't have any problems," Gault said, moving the pistol suggestively. "I trust you same as you trust me—long as things stay even. Hate to have you change your mind before we get out of sight."

Kingston's shoulders went down in resignation. "All right, goddammit, we're going. But like I said, if you're lying—"

"I'm not," Gault broke in coldly.

Silent then, he watched them drop their weapons into the dust, wheel, and move off, stumbling a little in high-heeled boots not made for walking. When they reached the first of the houses, Frank glanced to Lin.

"Hated to hand over that money. Was the only thing."

She shook her head. "Wasn't mine, anyway—and I'm glad to be rid of it . . . Are we really going to Tucson—both of us?"

He studied her closely. "What I had in mind, and hoped—if you're willing. Good chance I've got no job, and I'm sure not loaded with cash, but—"

She spurred her black up close to the buckskin, reached out her arms.

"That doesn't matter—none of it," she said as he gathered her in. "Only that you want me . . . I was afraid—"

"I'm the one who was afraid," he said. "Afraid I was losing you."

He turned his attention to the lawmen, now well down the street. They could ride on now. They'd hear no more from Kingston or Worley, or of a bank robbery in Colorado.

There was only the future to think of, and his need for certain now of a job. But he'd not worry about that . . . A man could always find a job, but a girl like Lin Cooper came along only once in a lifetime.